True's Love

By TL Clark

This book is dedicated to the one I love.
Without my incredibly supportive **husband** I
would never have had the courage to press that
magical publish button.

Thanks also to my wonderful proofreaders,
and to Robin Ludwig for the amazing cover.

And last but by no means least,
thank you lovely reader for buying this book.
Every review helps spur me on, and gives me
the strength to continue writing.

Thank you.

Chapter 1

Eurgh! Amanda had come about ten minutes ago, this guy was still nowhere close to finishing, and his head bobbing was really starting to irritate her; such a bad choice. How had she ended up here in this hotel room anyway? A whole series of bad choices. Her mind wandered…

OK. It was Kieran's fault; he'd started it all. She had been at Manchester University for a year before she'd met him (a year full of parties and fun). It was at one of those parties where she'd met him actually.

She was then nineteen years old, but had felt ready for the steady relationship that Kieran offered. He had been so lovely; black hair and brown eyes, and on the athletics team. She had thought herself madly in love with him, and did whatever he asked.

At first the sex was amazing, and they'd stayed up in her room for hours upon hours. She had started not socialising much, just so she could spend more time with him.

Then one day he produced a very small butt plug. She had been afraid at first, but with some coaxing and a lot of lube she had tried it, just to please him. He steadily trained her until one day he put himself in that sacred hole. It had hurt at first, but as she got used to it she started to enjoy it. He was very careful with her, and had seemed so loving.

That was the thing with Kieran, he always seemed very considerate. He would always open doors for her, take her coat. In short, behaved like a perfect gentleman.

Until one day she went to his room when her lesson had been cancelled. She caught him in bed with another girl, and that was that; the end of their seven month relationship.

She had hidden herself away for a fortnight, crying into her pillow and eating the obligatory consolation ice cream.

One of her friends had finally come to her rescue, and dragged her out to a party. She got absolutely mullered and ended up shagging some anonymous bloke in a pile of coats.

She was the one to walk away that night, and it gave her a huge sense of power. She decided then and there never to allow a man to ever hold dominion over her again. She was the boss of her.

What was that annoying noise? Oh right, it was her latest 'conquest' finally squeaking out his joy as he came at last.

She waited for him to fall asleep before going to the bathroom and showering really well. She glanced at her reflection in the mirror, and winced a little.

She barely recognised the superior brown gaze staring back at her through messy brown hair, with the jutting jawline of defiance. She quickly pulled on her clothes and sneaked out of the room.

The early hour meant it was freezing cold, not helped by the fact her hair was still wet. She hadn't wanted to wake the guy up by blow drying her hair, so it was clinging around her face and shoulders.

Fortunately, she managed to find a taxi quickly, and was soon back at her flat. She poured herself a G&T as she ran a bath.

This evening just made her feel dirty, and she wanted another wash to cleanse herself. As she lay there, surrounded by soapy suds she began to think about her life.

She was twenty six years old, and thanks to her regular exercise, was still a size 10.

Her exercise consisted of wicked sexual antics every weekend. All that sex really was a great workout routine.

She did some yoga in between to keep herself supple too. Plus, she could barely be bothered to cook, so she ate like a sparrow.

Her cascading chestnut hair and hazel eyes were her main allure though.

She really didn't struggle to find partners, but she had started to get a bit troubled about that lately.

Roughly speaking, she'd been sleeping around for seven years. Not that she minded that aspect; she loved sex, and really didn't want a relationship.

She was a strong, independent young woman. But she was beginning to wonder why she didn't charge for her time. No; that wasn't fair. She was not a prostitute. She chose her partners, and exactly what acts they did. And she had a good time. So, why was she feeling miserable?

She still hadn't quite managed to shake off her 'low' as she walked through her parents' front door the next morning, but she did manage to hide it behind a false smile, as she found herself hugged by her mother.

Although she drank on her nights out, she never drank to excess, so she was always aware of who she was going home with and what she was doing, so there was never a sign of bleary eyes or a hangover when she went to visit her folks.

"Darling, Amanda you're looking well. Brian, doesn't she look well?" chimed her mother.

This query was directed at her long suffering father, who merely nodded his agreement.

He was such a mild mannered man. He had recently retired, but his wife had him working hard on all the chores in the house to keep him occupied.

Her mother wasn't a beast. She just liked to keep her house in order.

It was a suburban dream house; one that was more show home than homely. But her heart was in the right place, and she was very affectionate.

Amanda was one of a rare breed; her childhood had been incredibly happy. She'd grown up in a safe, caring environment where she was nurtured. Perhaps she'd been protected from the world a little too much? There were no brothers or sisters, so she'd had her parents' undivided attention.

Amanda smiled as her mum put down the steaming plate of roast beef in front of her. This was her one wholesome square meal each week.

Her parents loved her to go round every Sunday. Her mum could fuss over the roast, and show her daughter how she still loved her, even though she was no longer at home.

And her dad would sit with her in the garden after she'd helped wash up. They had such wonderful philosophical conversations, whilst avoiding their own private lives.

Not that her dad was unhappy; he loved pottering around in his shed, and was still very fond of his wife after many years of marriage. He just wasn't one for discussing his private life.

This suited Amanda; she really didn't think her parents would approve of her 'modern lifestyle'. So he sat there in blissful ignorance, discussing the state of the world.

When it was time to leave, her mum hugged her close, and whispered her usual wish for her daughter to find a good man. She didn't push the matter though. She only ever wished the best for Amanda, and wanted to see her happy. She could sense there was an emptiness there, which Amanda always shrugged off.

This week though, Amanda couldn't quite shrug off the empty feeling her mum had picked up on. It was still there as she walked into work Monday morning.

She smiled her 'good morning' to security on her way in. Her life at work was very different. It reminded her of 'I Like It' by Narcotic Thrust. She hated her mundane 9-5 admin job, but it funded her weekends; a necessary evil on her path to good times.

But at least she had befriended Claire here. Claire had shown Amanda the ropes when she'd started here three years ago, and the pair were soon friends. She was one of Amanda's clubbing buddies.

She handed Claire the skinny latte she'd picked up for her on her way in.

"So, where did you end up Saturday?" Claire asked quietly as she sipped her coffee.

"Don't even ask. Did you see the tall blonde that I was talking to?"

"Yeaaah..."

"I ended up back in a hotel with him, but q'uel nightmare. He really didn't float my boat. He barely floated his own."

Claire pulled a scrunchy 'icky' face in sympathy. She wasn't as promiscuous as her friend, but admired her confidence, and loved hearing all the gossip.

"Besides, I'm on rest now until we go away."

"I can't believe it's come around so quickly. Two more weeks of work then… a week of fun in the sun. Ibiza here we come," squealed Claire.

The two girls grinned as they pinged on their PCs and started ploughing through emails.

As Amanda tried to get to sleep that night she started counting men, as one would normally count sheep…

Well, where to start? Kieran hadn't actually been her first. No, that was Simon's pleasure. He had been her short term sweetheart at senior school. He was nice, but it was the first time for both of them, so it had all been a bit awkward really.

Then Kieran was number two. Seven months of good loving there. He'd been like her own personal Kama Sutra.

He'd shown her how to be active whilst on the bottom, on top, on the side, back to front, standing up, lying down, pretty much any way at all. He certainly had been adventurous. But with him, her favourite had been to have him on top.

She had been so submissive then; wanting him to command her body at his whim. It had been such a good feeling.

He would start by slowly slowly peeling her clothes off her, nipping her skin as he went. He would make her senses sing at his touch.

Her top got delicately removed as he moved in to massage her breasts whilst kissing her. Those lips, so soft, so welcoming, so gentle but inquisitive. His tongue would seek hers as they lapped at each other. Their hands seeking the back of the others head, deepening their kiss, making them hungrier.

She'd practically melt in his arms as he removed his mouth from hers and gently lapped his way to her ear, circling her lobe round and round. Softly sucking at her ear, then blowing his sweet breath over where he'd just licked, sending delicious shivers down her spine.

He delved his tongue inside her ear then, sometimes making her have a mini orgasm even at that point. She was always certainly very wet for him by the time he started sucking his way down her throat, paying particular attention to her jugular.

She'd beg him for more, needing his body. Her nipples would find their way into his mouth for a minute or two.

The rain of kisses kept falling as he traversed her torso. Her skirt and knickers would quickly get discarded.

He would then turn his attention to her feet, and would suck her toes, sending her into a delirium. Her lust would only fire up more as he kissed and nipped his way up her ankles, her calves, then her inner thighs.

She would almost burst with anticipation as he came close to where she really wanted his tongue to go. She would grab his hair to urge him onwards, gasping with her desire. As his tongue finally found its mark she would burst into a bloom of fireworks, her orgasm shooting through her.

His tongue would carry on working its magic as his fingers joined the onslaught, gliding in and out of her, massaging her nub before diving in once more, sending her over the edge again.

As she was lost to the world he would climb on top of her, and look down at her with his dark eyes alight with his own passion, as his cock found home, uniting their bodies as one.

Oh, the sweet sensation of him filling her, that frantic friction as he slid himself in and out, her hips writhing up to him, allowing more access. Her legs would wrap around his back, drawing him forever deeper, making him groan with pleasure. He would quicken his pace as her hips rocked with increased vigour.

Her fingernails scratched his back as she clung on, forever wanting more.

Beads of sweat would run down their bodies as they continued their push and pull, going faster and faster, as they cried out for more and more, their flames growing higher and higher until they reached their peak and were consumed with their fire, climaxing in the most incredible all-consuming sensation of tightness gripping their entire bodies as he came with her and into her. Oh, the relief. The sweet sweet ecstasy.

And oh, how she missed him, even now. Amanda realised tears were falling down her cheeks as she recalled her favourite moments with Kieran.

She hadn't even been aware her hand had slipped under the bedclothes and she'd been touching herself as she thought of him. She'd actually just come.

She had been so lost in the memory. Treacherous body. Treacherous mind. This was ridiculous. She hadn't truly thought of him for years.

But this week had been so unsettling somehow, she realised she'd sought comfort in the last solid man she'd known.

Now she felt embarrassed. How could she have let herself think like that? It's not like she wanted him back. She really needed some good sex.

Maybe that guy at the weekend had just been that bad? Yep; all she needed was a good lay. But that would have to wait until holiday; Mother Nature was shortly due to pay a visit. That would explain the moody hormones too.

Right, this was so not helping with sleep. Back to counting men. Number 3; Mr Pile of Coats. Number 4; Greg (forgettable). Number 5; well, she'd stopped really trying to remember names from then on, to be honest. It was just a whole string of fucks. She didn't even know how many there had been.

She never brought them back here though. Her flat was her refuge from the world. She didn't need some weirdo stalker thanks. Amanda gave up on counting, and got up to get a glass of water. She really needed to snap out of this weird mood.

The week dragged on more than usual, especially as Amanda knew she wouldn't be going out that weekend.

That Friday she had a PJ night, and treated herself to a Chinese takeaway and a DVD. Brad Pitt appeared on her TV as she tucked into her gooey Sweet & Sour Chicken. Naturally, a glass of wine was helping to wash it down.

As she stared longingly at the screen, well the demi-god that was Brad with rippling tanned muscles, shaggy blonde hair and piercing blue eyes, oh; and a butt to dig your teeth into, she wished she could meet a guy like that.

But let's face it; they don't actually exist. She'd kissed enough frogs to know there were just frogs in the pond of life, and no princes.

The only men she knew with biceps like that were the gay ones who practically lived in the gym (more's the pity).

As she moped, she realised she'd got to the bottom of her takeaway tub. Time for the Minstrels then. The chocolate buttons melted in her mouth like raindrops from heaven. A bit more wine was required to wash away the chocolate.

She'd got home from work late, and by the time she'd showered, changed and reheated her takeaway time was getting on anyway. And with the added soporific effect of the wine she fell asleep on the sofa just as Brad was on the rampage.

She awoke next morning feeling a little better. The dreams of a blonde Adonis had probably helped. But she still couldn't resist visiting the scrapbook of her mind.

She'd had many fun times in the last few years. There was one night she had gone out in her best LBD, showing just enough cleavage, but not so much as to look like a Katie Price wannabe. Subtle makeup highlighted her gorgeous eyes.

One of the navy boats had just pulled into dock. She'd been with forces guys before; they were always good for a laugh. They worked so hard, but needed to play even harder to work off the stress of serving their Queen and country. And their bodies were finely tuned machines, ready for action. Oh; those muscles.

She met Gary and Ethan in a dark, heaving nightclub. It was a fairly normal night; music thumping, a couple of vodkas pounding through her veins as she writhed on the dance floor amongst the throbbing masses, sweaty bodies all colliding.

One of the sweaty bodies next to Amanda was Ethan. He had a glint in those wild blue eyes as he accidentally on purpose grinded against her. She admired the view and grinded back.

He exuded such confidence; the look that flitted across his face was one of 'you want me as much as I want you, and we're gonna do it tonight'.

Amanda loved this bit; the bump and grind of hello. Ethan was clearly fit.

The crowd raised up a, "whoop whoop" in time with the music. They both chorused their "whoop whoop" response, and smiled at each other.

As they jumped around Amanda suddenly felt another body at her back, and had a moment of panic. She gasped as she was suddenly surrounded by two huge men, and not just the one. But Ethan moved in to kiss her, and somehow she knew she was safe.

He yelled and motioned with his hands whether she wanted to get out of there. She texted Claire on her way out to let her friend know where she was going (or where she hoped she was going, at least). The other bloke followed them out of the club.

"I'm Ethan. This is my friend Gary. Do you want to go get a drink?"

"Yeah. The hotel down the road has a nice quiet bar where we can talk," Amanda pointed in the general direction and started walking.

"I'm Amanda by the way."

"Hi Amanda. I'm very pleased to meet you," Ethan drawled.

"Ummm... I have a friend I can call, if Gary would like company?"

"We wouldn't want to spoil the party now, would we?" Ethan purred, with a grin filled with wickedness.

Oooookaaaay. So, their intentions were quite clear. Was she up for two guys at once? Thanks to Kieran's antics she knew she was capable. She was mulling the idea over as they reached the bar entrance.

"What you drinking?" Kieran asked her.

"Vodka and Coke, please."

She watched carefully as it was poured, and grabbed the glass herself. If she was going to do this she would, but she didn't want to get drugged and forced.

Ethan made no motion towards her glass anyway. They went to sit down in a quiet corner, and Ethan sidled up to her on the 'comfy seat', and planted a quick kiss on her plump lips.

"I want you," he whispered softly.

"I want you too," she replied with only a hint of hesitation, and a lot of breathiness.

"Is it OK for my friend to join us?"

Yep. No confusion there. She supposed that guys on ships spent so much time together, they saw each other naked a lot, so no need for embarrassment there. Still, it was a bit weird. Could be good? She took another gulp of her vodka and Coke.

"I guess."

"We'll take it slow. You don't have to do anything you don't want to do. And say stop any time OK?"

"OK."

"I'm going to leave you here with Gary for a minute. I'll go get a couple of rooms."

He returned ten minutes later and handed Gary the spare key to one room. Ethan then took Amanda's hand to help her to her feet.

"OK?" he checked.

Amanda was so nervous she could only nod as she was led to the lifts. Once inside he stepped in close and brushed her cheek softly before kissing her again, but this time it grew in intensity.

By the time the doors pinged open she was panting. This was so hot. He led her to his room, and explained Gary would be up soon, he was just being subtle. She thought she heard herself mutter about his friend not saying much, but she sounded miles away.

They stepped into the room, and Ethan switched on a dull side light; just enough illumination to take away the eeriness of the dark, but not so much as to be harsh.

He bent down for another kiss, his tongue caressing hers, his hands on her hips. She felt the moistness and heat between her legs. She wanted him. She grabbed onto his back and pulled him close enough to feel his erection come into contact with her.

She still needed an element of control in this. She started to unbutton his shirt, revealing toned muscles. He smiled down at her lasciviously as he shrugged his shirt off.

She undid his trousers; whoah! He was going commando (ironically). His erection stood out proudly as she got him to step out of his trousers. She took it in her hands and began to stroke in slow steady movements, making him hiss through his teeth.

"Steady," he warned.

There was a noise at the door, as Gary let himself in with the spare key card.

"You started without me?" Gary asked in mock concern, and stalked up to Amanda.

"Hi again," he breathed, and kissed her.

He was even better at that than Ethan was. He hitched up her dress not hesitating with politeness. His fingers slipped past her underwear, and immediately found that she was wet and ready. He slid his fingers against her, slowly at first. She moaned into his mouth.

"You like that, baby?"

"Mmmm...."

"Tell me what you want."

When she couldn't reply he carried on with his questions, "You want me to fuck you?"

"Ah haa."

He rubbed her harder.

"You want my cock here?"

"Aaaahhhh," she moaned, verge of climaxing.

"Yeah. You want me inside you. You want to feel me going in and out of here."

As he said this two of his fingers slid in and out of her. She orgasmed around his fingers with a gasp. She clung on to him as he held onto her with his free arm.

He gently lowered her down on her back onto the bed. He tugged her knickers off. Ethan was the other side and was pulling her dress off over her head. He took her bra off her. She was now completely naked and at their mercy.

Ethan moved to the bottom of the bed and made his way up, parting her thighs, going straight in to lap the length of her labia.

"You taste so sweet" he gasped before continuing to lick her.

His tongue was so warm and soft, and he teased her with it mercilessly. When she was about to explode with frustration he took her in his mouth and sucked hard, taking her over the brink.

Gary had been watching, and had taken himself in hand, excited at the spectacle in front of him.

Gary rolled onto the bed next to Amanda.

"Come here, sweetie," he commanded.

She happily straddled him, and reached for the clubbing bag on the bedside table and reached in for a condom.

"Only once we get you safe." she said as she rolled it on him.

She grabbed another packet and put it on Ethan who had positioned himself out of the way.

"You too."

Her clubbing bag was always well equipped; condoms, mobile phone, mini lube, mini deodorant, a compact brush, wet wipes and a lipstick as well as a small purse and her keys.

She now chucked the lube at Ethan, as she mounted Gary, whom she was now in control of.

"You like that, baby? You want your cock there?" she teased as she pumped up and down.

His moans of pleasure were exactly what she wanted. Ethan squirted the lube and began rubbing in all the right places. He knelt up behind her as she leaned forward enough to give him full access.

He gently started pushing his way inside of her. She winced a little, but Gary in her other hole was enough of a happy distraction.

Before long all three were moving together in a steady rhythm. She could feel both of them, solid and thrusting in and out of her, building their friction. She moved faster, and they matched her. More and more.

Ethan reached round to squeeze her nipples, Gary reached down and caressed her clitoris. So many sensations. Oh, the ecstasy. Her entire body was alive with electricity, humming with excitement.

She rubbed herself against Gary's finger as she rocked her body up and down. She was the first to find her release, and the boys followed closely behind, all surging with the power of their orgasms. Groaning their relief. They all collapsed in a big heap of flesh on the bed.

Gary was the first to get up to go to the bathroom. Ethan seized the opportunity to kiss Amanda and whisper his gratitude. When Gary came back Amanda went to take a quick shower. When she came back Ethan was alone in the bed.

"Gary's gone to sleep next door."

"Oh."

She was a bit disappointed he hadn't even said goodbye.

"I'll be heading off myself anyway."

"You don't have to go, you know." He said as he made a gap under the covers for her, and raised an eyebrow at her.

"Really?"

She was surprised he had any energy left, quite frankly. But she got in to join him.

"I love your body Amanda. And I didn't get to try this," he muttered in her ear as he reached down between her legs.

He stroked her as he nibbled her neck. He seemed oddly caring like this. She rolled onto her back, and passed him a fresh condom. He moved between her legs, and kissed her longingly.

He stroked her cheek gently and breathed in the scent of her hair. He lowered himself into her, taking care not to hurt her after the rigours she'd just gone through.

He made love to her slowly and languorously. Her body arched in response to his caring caress. When they came it was together this time and he laid his head down next to hers whilst he composed himself.

He kissed her once more as he rolled onto his side. He rubbed his hand down her body, taking in the sensation of her soft silky skin. He looked really young as he fell asleep.

Amanda wondered how such young men could be sent out to fight. He had looked almost twice his age in that club. Now she realised he couldn't be any older than nineteen.

She felt slightly guilty as she did her disappearing act out of that room. She had a nasty feeling he would have wanted more from her than she could give.

But she couldn't have a relationship with someone who was absent so often and for so long. The paranoia would have driven her mad. And she was just all about the fun, baby. So she had scurried back to the refuge of her home.

Amanda smiled as she came out of her daydream. OK; maybe not *all* the buff, good looking types were gay, but they were rare.

That had possibly been the best night of her life. But it was no good looking back. She could only move forward. And right now she needed to get up and eat breakfast.

Chapter 2

The time passed slowly in the monotony of the daily grind of the office. But eventually, Claire and Amanda were at the airport, about to board the plane to Ibiza.

Nervousness and excitement hung in the air between the two girls like a fog. They both really needed a break, and even Claire was hoping to get laid. Her revealing clubbing dresses were all packed, as were her tankinis (to hide her size 12 figure around the pool during the day).

She couldn't help comparing herself to Amanda, who was only a size 10. But that was your mid-twenties for you; this was the start of the weight gain. At least she had managed to tone up a bit thanks to her Wii Fit.

She usually only slept with guys she was in a relationship with, but she was currently in between boyfriends, so was hoping to break the dry spell abroad. Different country; different rules.

The girls tramped down the walkway to the plane in their flipflops, and were directed to their seats.

They settled down and watched the other passengers do likewise. It always reminded Amanda of a shoal of fish; all jimmying for the best position, as the passengers scurried around one another, shoving their luggage into the overhead lockers.

It was the same the other end too; all rushing to be the first off despite the fact they all knew there'd be a long wait at the baggage carousel anyway.

Claire held onto Amanda's hand as the engines started rumbling and the wings flexed as they backed away from the terminal. She was a nervous passenger, and the friendly safety video overhead did nothing to calm her nerves.

Amanda squeezed back and tried to distract her friend. She pulled out the hip flask of vodka and orange juice she'd stashed in the seat pocket in front of her, and passed it to Claire, who took a grateful sip, but still noted the emergency exits were 'here, here and here' though.

After a wait at the end of the runway the engines started roaring fully, and the vibrations went through the seats, and there were all sorts of bing-bong noises as the captain presumably did his final checks, and ordered the cabin crew to take their positions for take-off.

Amanda felt the roar quite exciting as they trundled up the runway, gathering speed with a few bumps along the way. Then with an almighty effort the plane was airborne. Their ears popped as they climbed higher and higher into the clouds.

Poor Claire was taking the deep breaths of a woman in labour. She felt another squeeze on her hand. Finally they were at the correct altitude, and levelled off. Claire took another sip, and relaxed. They were truly on their way. Freedom for a week.

Just a few short hours later they touched down, with Claire's hand clutching onto Amanda's, grateful they'd got to their destination in one piece.

And now they were getting out of the plane. The heat-wave hit them as they stepped through the door and onto the metal steps which took them down onto the tarmac. Yes, they had arrived; bliss.

There was the usual bustle through customs and baggage reclaim, but gradually they were herded through like cattle and onto the courtesy bus to take them to their resort.

They pulled up at the cheap and cheerful hotel in the centre of Ibiza Town. Pacha nightclub was within walking distance, and Claire's friend had scored them some tickets for tomorrow night. They couldn't wait.

Hot and tired from travelling the girls went straight up to their rooms. They had opted for a room each as it was cheap enough; no worrying about snoring or who they brought back for them.

Their rooms were next door to each other, and they knew they'd be in each other's rooms getting ready etc.

For now, it was time for a quick shower and nap before preparing for their first night out in the town. Travelling was tiring, and they were planning a very long night. Beauty sleep was required.

Claire was the one to knock on Amanda's door first, asking to share her hair straighteners, and had her makeup bag in hand. Gold sparkle was the choice for eye makeup tonight, and sultry dark red lipstick. Finished with a hint of eyeliner and plenty of mascara and they were done.

Skimpy dresses in place, they topped up with some duty free alcohol purchased en route. Slightly tipsy already, the pair started trotting along the road to the first nightclub they could find.

The clubs and streets were already heaving with party-goers, and the promoters were in situ enticing people in. Claire and Amanda shoved their way in past writhing bodies to get to the bar.

Drink bottles in hand they delved into the throng. The darkness was interrupted by laser lights beaming through the darkness. The music was pumping, the whole place was alive with the beat, strangers mingling together in the fervour of the night.

It wasn't long before Amanda found some guy's tongue in her mouth. But he wasn't her type so she left it at that. Claire was looking on with a bemused smile as her friend made her way back to her, pulling a look of disapproval, making them both giggle.

On they danced and drank, feeling the rhythm pound through them, their bodies reacting in kind. Hours passed liked minutes. For a moment, it looked like Claire was going to pull, but she declared the guy's kissing abilities akin to those of a haddock.

A little worse for wear, the girls staggered back to their hotel in the early morning. It was a tame start, but it held promise.

The girls limped out of bed about midday, and went in search for coffee and carbs. Fortunately, they didn't have to wander too far before they found a store. They were feeling quite delicate after consuming a little too much alcohol last night.

They took their treasure back to the sun loungers by the small pool, where they lounged in the sun like lizards. They weren't the only ones; there were many sorry looking people strewn around the pool.

They got chatting to some nice looking guys. They invited them to a good club they'd discovered, but the girls declined, already having Pacha plans.

That night they grabbed some chips on their way to Pacha, munching as they made their way to their ultimate goal.

They gained admittance, and it was like walking into the holy grail of nightclubs. It was enormous, and had a few different rooms to explore, but the girls ended up in the main room.

The live DJs were epic. The talent wasn't so bad here either. But just as Amanda was halfway through the night, and having snagged a hunny, was merrily kissing him, Claire tapped her on the shoulder looking a bit green.

Amanda immediately escorted her friend outside, just in time to hold her hair back for her whilst she heaved into the road. Too much heat, not enough food and too much alcohol had Claire in a bad way pretty quickly.

Once she was satisfied her friend had finished she hobbled her over to a nearby wall so she could sit down. As she sat down herself she felt a cool bottle of water being slipped into her hand. She looked up with alarm at a dazzling pair of blue eyes framed by a beautiful chiselled jaw and shaggy blonde hair.

It was the man from her Brad Pitt-but-not dream. She looked down at the bottle in her hand incredulously, not sure she should trust her senses. Maybe she wasn't too far behind Claire after all? But no, the Adonis mirage spoke.

"It's OK. It's still sealed," said the vision, the street light behind him shining a halo around his head.

"Ah. Yeah. Thanks," Amanda stuttered.

"Excuse me."

It was then, as he turned away that Amanda realised the demigod had his own charge who was also upchucking into the road.

She opened the bottle of water and made Claire take a few sips. Mr Blonde aimed his mate at the wall too. Amanda stood up to make room.

"Popular place," she said with a shy giggle.

"Yeah, mum's spaghetti junction, eh?" his voice had the hint of an accent.

"Thanks for the water."

"It was nothing. I had a spare."

She wanted to say anything just to keep him talking, just so she could hear his voice. But for once she couldn't think of anything, especially as he was glowering at his friend, who was groaning in unison with hers. There was an odd sort of communication going on between those two.

"Don't you just hate it when your night gets cut short like this?" she asked in what she hoped sounded like a sympathetic voice.

"Not really. No. I wasn't having fun anyway. This way I get a quiet night."

"Oh."

"Sorry. I don't mean to take out my bad mood on you. That was rude. It's just… well, it's complicated."

"That's OK. No explanations needed."

"Are you OK to get back to your hotel?"

"Yeah thanks. Do you want to share a taxi?"

Mr Yummy smiled a little, and oh, what fine white teeth he had. And oh, what amazing light shone from those baby blues. Amanda was melting as she heard him reply.

"No thank you. Our hotel is near."

Bugger it (Amanda thought).

"Well. It was nice meeting you," she said meekly (most uncharacteristic for her).

"You're leaving already? Is she up to a car journey?" he motioned towards Claire, who now had an arm around the other worse-for-wear.

"I think she'll be fine. I just need to get her back to her bed."

There was a moment of uncertainty as a frown flickered across his face. He wasn't really sure what he was doing or why. The words just tumbled out of his mouth, as if driven by an unseen force.

"This may be forward, but would you like to join me for breakfast?"

"Are you asking me back to your room for the night? Because I need to look after my friend right now."

He shook his head, a look of sorrow passing over his fantastic features.

"No. I was asking you for actual breakfast. To meet me in the morning, as these two sleep off their headaches."

"Oh. That's very nice of you…" she trailed off, realising she didn't know his name.

"Michael," he offered.

"Hmph. Doesn't sound very Russian."

"Who said I was Russian?" Michael asked, emphasising his accent.

"Umm… sorry. It's just you sounded as if…"

"Relax, pretty one. You are right. Not that many have the courage to ask outright like that. My name is actually Mikhail, but it got changed when people couldn't pronounce it properly enough for my father."

"Well, it was very nice to meet you Mikhail."

"Very nice. My name falls from your lips like a summer breeze. But you still have not told me your name."

"Sorry. I'm Amanda. And Bride of Chucky over there is Claire."

"So Amanda, may I buy you breakfast?"

"Thanks, but I'm going to have to say no."

"Ouch."

"I don't mean to hurt your feelings."

"I confess to being a little hurt. I saw you in there. You didn't seem so shy then."

"Just who do you think you are, standing there insulting me? Just because I said no. Good looks will only take you so far, you know."

'Actually, you're a little too gorgeous for me, and I'm scared of how you're making me feel, especially as I may forgive you anything with you looking at me like that,' she added in her head.

"OK. I can take a hint."

He really had no idea why he was asking her anyway. He was being irrational. He had work to do. He didn't have time for frivolous distractions, no matter how gorgeous they were. He took her hand in his and bowed as he kissed it.

"Thank you for keeping me company anyway. But please, Amanda. You must be careful."

"Careful?"

"It's not my place. I'm sorry. But I saw you on the dance floor. You are far too attractive to be so reckless."

"Alright. Thanks dad," she retorted huffily.

"Come on you," she said, dragging Claire to her feet.

"Say goodnight to your new friend."

"Niiiighhht…" Claire slurred.

"Night, Michael. Thanks again for the water," Amanda said over her shoulder whilst supporting up her friend.

But as she turned to leave she felt a slip of paper get placed in her hand.

"In case you change your mind?"

He looked as hopeful as a puppy asking to be cuddled. And with that he propped up his friend and started walking him up the road.

The girls limped in the opposite direction in search for a taxi.

Amanda dumped Claire on her bed, and put the remaining water on the bedside table for her. She then went into her own room and slumped herself on her own bed.

Her hand was still clutching Michael's phone number. He really had been gorgeous. And kind. And oh, that voice; softly touched by his Russian accent in the distance.

So, why was she not going to breakfast? Maybe that was the problem? If he had asked her *for breakfast* in the 'I'm gonna shag you until sunrise' sense she'd be there in his room right now. But going out for a meal, even just breakfast felt like a date.

She didn't do dates. Nope. Strong independent woman right here. Certainly doesn't need a man complicating her life. Nope siree. No vacancy for a 5ft 9″, beautiful, blonde, velvet voiced, blue eyed, kind man.

What was she so afraid of? She didn't know him. He could be an axe murderer for all she knew. Yeah, an axe murderer handing out free bottles of water.

Oh, it was hopeless. She was just being a complete wuss puss. Fine. But at least her heart wouldn't get torn to shreds again.

She woke up too early to disturb Claire. She could really do with her friend right now, but she put her swimsuit on instead. She needed to swim off some junk food anyway. And OK, try to exercise some of her frustration out too.

She got down to the pool and dived in. The cool rush of the water jolted her into action. Her front crawl action was fast and furious, as if she was swimming away from a shark that was chasing her.

As she stopped at last in the shallow end to catch her breath a pair of feet appeared in her vision. It was one of the boys they had chatted to yesterday.

"So, how was Pacha?"

"Not as good as I'd hoped. Claire got sick so we came home early."

"Aww. That's a shame. You up to coming out with Shane and me tonight instead? Save on taxi fare?"

"Yeah. Sure. Meet you in reception tonight?"

"Cool. It's a date."

Amanda's heart stopped at the phrase, but she knew this wasn't that kind of date. This was heading to the same club together, and if things went well they'd end up back at the hotel together, but that was it. No butterflies fluttering here. Just good honest sex. This she could handle.

Amanda knew when Claire was awake when she heard a chair being scraped out of the way, and a loud groan. She went and knocked, armed with more water.

"How you feeling?"

"Like someone's got a pick axe hacking into my brain."

"Here, drink this," Amanda said, shoving the bottle of water at Claire.

"Cheers."

After taking a grateful gulp she tried asking, "How was breakfast?"

"Breakfast?"

"Yeah. There was a gorgeous bloke, right?"

"Oh him. No, I didn't go."

"What? Why? Tall, blonde and handsome not your type?"

"He just wanted actual breakfast. I didn't feel like it."

"Amanda."

"Don't Amanda me. Please. It's just…"

"Hey. It's your life. I don't think I'd have been able to turn him down though."

"I don't think you would have been able to string a sentence together. You were hammered."

"Mmm. Yeah, sorry. I'll take it easier tonight."

"Oh; that reminds me. The poolside blokes asked us to go to that club tonight."

"Oh, you'll say yes to *them*?"

"They're less complicated."

"Fine. Fine."

"Come on. Shove some clothes on. We need to find coffee and something to eat. And then we need to keep you in the shade."

"OK mum."

Amanda felt a tinge of sadness as she thought of accusing Michael of being dad-like last night. Oh well, even if she did want to change her mind there'd be no coming back from that.

After finding refreshments the girls went to a mini mart and found some snacks, and spent the day in the cool air conditioning of their room.

Claire needed some serious recuperation after the previous night. They flicked through the English magazines they'd brought with them, and bitched about the celebrities contained therein, as they munched their way through all sorts of unhealthy chocolate, crisps, sweets and fizzy drinks. The combination of Fanta and Coke was particularly refreshing.

Feeling much more human, Claire was ready for another night on the town. She and Amanda met Shane and Jordan in reception as promised, and the four headed off into the night.

Amanda's stomach lurched as they neared Pacha, but relaxed as they went up the road a bit further to a different club. To be fair, it was a pretty good choice. The music was right, and the crowd was buzzing.

They all got pulled into the mass and were soon throwing down shapes with the best of them. But as Claire and Amanda returned from a loo break the lads were groping some other bints instead. Great. A week of sex, eh? She had better luck at home; what a let-down. Oh well. Another vodka should help.

The bar was just a crush of people, but they eventually got served. As the girls returned to the throng Amanda couldn't help but think of Michael's words of warning. Who was he to tell her what to do anyway? She *was* careful thanks! With that she was determined not to get disappointed tonight.

She scanned the talent, and homed in on her victim. Yeah; not too young, not too old. Just enough confidence to handle himself, but not so much that she couldn't handle him. Trim, brown hair, brown eyes. Average Joe, here we go.

Amanda sidled up to her target and started dancing near him, letting her eyes meet his. She could practically hear her fishing reel wind in as he came closer. They were soon gyrating their hips together.

She manoeuvred them into a suitably dark corner. The music was pumping through her veins. As he reached his hands round to grope her arse she snogged him full on. He raised an eyebrow in slight surprise but returned the kiss, their tongues whirling and colliding.

"Ahhh yeah," he groaned.

"Yeah. You want me?"

"Ohhh yeeeahh,"

"Here?"

"Now."

She reached down and unzipped his flies. His cock sprang forth between them, but she was careful to conceal it with her dress. She took a condom out of her bag and surreptitiously slid it on him, making sure their bodies were really close.

"This is really hot," he gasped as she slid a leg up to his hip and guided him in.

Her back was against a wall, and he pushed his way in. Their kiss got deeper and more passionate. The crowd danced around them, oblivious to what was going on. The thought that one of those people could turn around and see what they were doing at any moment was a real turn on.

The bass gave them their rhythm as they thrust themselves together. She gripped onto his arse, trying to get more purchase. She wanted this. She needed this. They were sweaty from dancing already, but their heat together intensified, making them sticky.

Her mouth was all over his as she rocked her hips, pulling down on her raised leg, pulling, pushing, more. He kept up his onslaught, and pushed harder.

"Ahh," she gasped as she climaxed just before he did.

Oh the sweet relief of a quickie on the dance floor. She gave Mr Anonymous a quick peck as she walked off to find Claire. They went to the toilets together so Amanda could freshen up, but also so Claire could get details.

"Did you really just do that guy?"

"Yeah."

"Right there on the dance floor. Oh...my...god...!"

"Yep. That was really hot."

But even as she said it she felt empty, the adrenalin retreating already. Yeah, it was horny as fuck, but was it truly satisfying?

"Guess we need to find another club then?" asked Claire.

"Yeah, it'd be just awkward if we just stayed here."

As the girls slid out into the night they started walking down the street, but not finding anything promising, they veered off down a side street. It was quite dark but there were people not too far away. The trouble was they had no idea where they were going.

"Amanda. This doesn't look right. Maybe we should just head back?" Claire said as they wandered further.

Just as Amanda was about to agree with her a shadowy figure jumped out in front of them.

"Money. NOW," a Spanish voice commanded.

He was pointing a knife at them. But they were too horrified to move.

"NOW!" he yelled again.

There was a blur, and a clatter of metal as the knife dropped to the ground. What the fuck?

"Hey arsehole," a slightly Russian voice said with menace.

The attacker spun round to see where the voice had come from, only to find a fist come into contact with his jaw, a second before a foot landed in his stomach, doubling him over. As he was bent at the waist a knee came up to meet his chin. And a foot swiped out his now very unsteady legs.

Michael talked into his sleeve before turning his attention to a very scared Amanda and Claire. But fear soon turns to anger.

"What the fuck are you doing?" hissed Amanda.

"Saving your sorry life. Errr…thank you? You're welcome."

"Oh yes, thank you very much for stalking me."

He took her arm and pulled her up the street back in the direction of the main road, as a suited and booted man ran up the alley to the prostrate assailant.

"And who's he; one of your henchmen?"

"I wasn't stalking you. I left my client to come to your aid. Now, please excuse me and I'll get back to my job if I still have one."

"Your client?"

"Yeah. The guy I'm paid to protect, alright? Do I have your permission to dismiss myself?"

"Ah yeah. Sure. Sorry."

"Don't be sorry. Be better. Look, you'd better get out of here."

"But won't the police want to take a statement?"

"We've got it covered. Look; there's a taxi rank up there. It's crowded along here, you'll be safe."

The girls climbed into a taxi and barely breathed until they got back to Amanda's room. They started tucking into the rest of the duty free vodka, just as a medicinal measure.

"I can't believe we were attacked like that," Claire shrilled, still visibly shaken.

"No. Nor can I."

Amanda was quiet, almost sullen.

"Was that really the same guy from last night?"

"Yeah, it was. Playing witness to me at my most stupid."

"Stupid? No. We just walked into a bad area. It could've happened to anyone."

"Yeah, but it happened to us. And now he knows I'm gobby *and* stupid."

"I still disagree with the stupid, but you were rather rude to him. He had just saved our lives."

"No. I know. I was just so shocked, and he was the last person I expected to see. After having some guy jump out at me, my mind was racing on the negative."

"What do you care anyway? Not like you were interested in him."

"No. Guess not."

"Amanda. You weren't interested in him, were you?"

"No. Of course not. Maybe. I don't know."

"The great Amanda Trueman doesn't do dates, remember?"

"Maybe the not-so-great Amanda was starting to get swayed."

"Noooo!"

"I said maybe. It's ridiculous really. I don't know the first thing about him."

"Well, he's tall, blonde and yummy. And is some sort of bodyguard or henchman," Claire teased.

"Yeah. What was that?"

"Beats me. Hot though."

"I don't need protecting. And I hate that he now thinks I do."

"So, don't see him again?"

"Well, that will be fairly easy after tonight."

Claire leaned in to give her friend a hug. She'd never seen her like this. For all her protestations she seemed really vulnerable right now.

Alone in bed after Claire had shuffled into her room to sleep off the effects of the night, Amanda was lying awake. She was thinking of a blonde hero, dashing out of nowhere like Superman to save her. She murmured softly as her hand disappeared under the sheets.

Chapter 3

Meanwhile, Michael had got back to his own room, having deposited his client safely back in his room, after having partied the rest of the night away.

Michael had been uneasy allowing him to continue, but Hugo had insisted on 'having fun'. Bloody spoiled rich kid, but he was the boss. Besides, Mark had seen to the would-be mugger quickly and was back 'on the door'.

Michael had spoken to the club owner previously, and had gained consent to place his assistant as a doorman (undercover). The owner had been more than happy to have an extra pair of hands for free, as long as he followed the rules of the house, of course.

Good job he had taken that step; Mark had come in handy when Amanda had wandered down that dark alley. What had she been thinking, for heaven's sake? Ditzy bint.

But there was something captivating about her. He hadn't been able to get her out of his head ever since he'd first seen her enter Pacha. Even when he'd witnessed her getting off with every Tom, Dick and Harry; everyone except him.

Getting the brush off from her had wounded his ego a bit. He hadn't had time to date properly in years, so maybe his technique was somewhat lacking? To be honest, he didn't have time for it now.

Hugo was a real handful at the best of times. His father was really overbearing though, so he couldn't blame the kid for wanting to blow off steam once he was free for a few weeks. His father was a very rich, very powerful man, and had clearly ticked off some people on his climb up the business ladder, and there had been many death threats on him and his family.

Michael couldn't blame the guy for being protective after that. Most of the threats were naturally from relatively harmless freaks, but then one had gained access to the grounds of the family home and set fire to the shrubs which lined the drive. Thankfully that's all he'd done, but it had scared Hugo's father enough to step up his security, and employ the specialist services of Michael.

At home, poor Hugo wasn't allowed out of the grounds without his hired help, which naturally irked the twenty-two year old. Michael had been chosen, not only for his proven track record, but also because he had a young face, and his image made him just look like a friend. It was as subtle as he could manage. But naturally, Hugo still resented it.

Mark was babysitting now as Hugo slept in the room next door. Michael was exhausted, having done four very long shifts back-to-back. He was giving himself tomorrow off, having enough resources to cover Hugo's comings and goings.

Fortunately he was quiet enough during the day anyway, barely leaving the grounds of the swanky hotel. It was just opposite Pacha, so very handy for Hugo, given that's where he wanted to spend most nights.

He'd heard about the infamous parties, so naturally wanted to go. Michael would have loved it if he wasn't on duty, but he couldn't drink and had to keep his wits about him all the time, so it was just strained.

The little punk couldn't hold his alcohol, and of course didn't listen to his advice. Mind you, it was handy the other night, when he'd managed to hoof him outside as he saw Amanda disappear out the door.

Why was he mooning over this girl? He was practically married to his job. He was resigned to that. Girlfriends could be a security risk, and at best, damned inconvenient. She'd make demands on his time, when it was impossible as he had to be on duty or standby.

Girls didn't exactly appreciate coming second. He had tried and epically failed a couple of times. Besides, he didn't know which *country* he was going to end up in next let alone which town.

Thanks to his heritage, he spoke several languages. He had been born in Russia to a Russian father and an English mother. They'd left Moscow when he was four years old though, as his father had got a promising teaching job in England.

His mother was a nurse, but had been homesick for years, so off they went. The kids at school had teased him because of his accent, so he'd tried to drop as much of it as he could.

He was lucky his mum had spoken English to him all his life, so he'd grown up bi-lingual. His father was a foreign languages teacher, and had encouraged his son to learn French. Michael had found a natural talent, and had gone on to pursue an interest in German, Spanish and Italian.

He studied foreign languages at University, which had then led to him spending time abroad. He'd loved experiencing different cultures. To tide him over at uni, he'd bagged a part-time job as a bouncer, and happily combined the two to help him travel round the world.

He loved his job, and the freedom it gave him. Having gotten into close personal protection, he'd started being able to command higher fees, especially from the likes of his current client.

As a result, he had quite a lot of savings at just thirty years old. But then, he didn't own a house (he was always flitting from job to job), and had very low overheads generally.

He was starting to wonder what good it was though, having all this money but never getting to actually enjoy it. But it all added to the pension fund. He couldn't keep this lifestyle up forever.

Last year he'd been recruited for a gig on a private yacht. And by yacht, the client had meant floating hotel. The thing was huge (classed as a super/luxury yacht). He'd spent all summer cruising around the Med, guarding the owner. It was more for show than effect really. The guy liked to look flash.

They'd even dropped in at Monaco for the Grand Prix. Bit of a blast from the past for Michael; he'd done a few events, and this circuit was one he'd had the privilege of guarding.

It made him laugh, the way the uber rich all had to outdo each other at these events. 'I've got the biggest yacht.' 'Yeah, but I have the skinniest, youngest model on mine.' Quite frankly it was all a bit nauseating; too much like a penis sizing competition (all participants being less than well endowed).

But he was paid to protect, not to have an opinion, so he bit his tongue. Especially as he got great food and great perks out of all their show boating.

Mark had been one of his employees for a few years now, but he was more than that. He'd become a trusted friend. A natural progression really; having to watch each other's backs all the time kind of made you bond quickly. It helped that Mark had the same nomadic dreams as Michael. He was happy to tag along anywhere their jobs took them.

So this was his life; happy as Larry. He really didn't need the complication of anything even vaguely approaching a girlfriend. Especially not some gobby tart.

But man, those hazel eyes of hers did something to him. They bared a soul that cried out to him. Man up Mr Alkaev. Jees, like grow a pair. He wasn't some love sick teenager for chrissakes. Maybe it was the way she seemed strong yet vulnerable all at once.

He was sort of trained to find those in need of protection, and man, he really wanted to protect her. He could lock her in his bedroom safe from the world for a month, shielding her with his body.

When Hugo had the first signs of turning green tonight he'd dragged him outside to get fresh air before he even thought about being sick again. That was just so humiliating; it was pathetic.

As they got out of the crowd he'd seen her. Drawn to Amanda like a sixth sense. He'd been tempted to go and talk to her straight away. He knew it would only have earned him another knock back though, and Hugo would have sulked about being left all alone (diddums).

But then as he watched her snakelike hips saunter up the road she'd disappeared into that alley. His hair stood up on the back of his neck and he'd shoved Hugo at Mark like a sack of spuds, as he took flight after Amanda.

As he got close he heard the demand for money, and saw the girls stunned like rabbits caught in headlights. That punk was going to get stabby if they didn't do something. With no time to think, he had acted on impulse and kicked the weapon out of that shit's hand and dragged his attention away from the girls.

Beating the crap out the lowlife had been cathartic. He'd needed to get some pent up frustration out, and he had been the perfect punch bag.

He'd called Mark as backup before he could get too carried away though. Hugo had been safe enough with the real doorman briefly. But boy, had he copped it when he got back to him. Such a whiny little shit.

"How dare you abandon me like that?" and "What the hell do I pay you for?" had strewn out of his mouth like poison. Michael was in no mood to humour him. He'd known exactly where his charge was at all times, and that he was safe. No way would he let anything happen to him. But then, he had gone running after a bit of skirt, hadn't he? Wow; that was unprofessional. Little Shit had a point.

And what had he got for saving her life? A round of abuse from her *and* his client. Great night. Fortunately, Hugo had been too drunk to really care very much, and once he'd gotten back inside the club he was happily trying to grope girls. What a shmuck.

As for Amanda? Actually, finding she had that much spunk was kinda sexy. Admittedly, it was mostly a kneejerk reaction to having been frozen in terror and shock.

But even when they had previously met she'd held her own, hadn't she? Bright eyes sparking when he'd wounded her pride.

Heaven help him, those eyes. Those sweet looking lips. What he'd give just for one taste. To be able to kiss her like that oik had in the club. To pull her close, to invade her mouth with his tongue, to stroke her hair, to inhale her scent.

How he longed to see what was under that dress, to caress her tits with his tongue, to part those supple thighs.

His hand was stroking his cock in long fluid movements now, as he laid naked on his bed. To see her smile up at him as he laid himself upon her, burying his dick into her. To make her gasp, to see her sweat.

He needed to know how she felt, how slick she would be as he drove himself in and out of her. He wanted to see her arch her back as he pleasured her.

Meanwhile, Amanda's thoughts were running along very similar lines. She was thinking of her blonde Superman lying helpless on her bed as she straddled him.

She wanted to wipe that silly smirk off his face. Judging her. Ha. Judge this! Lie back and see just how strong she could really be. She wanted to have him begging for her. And just as he was pleading, then and only then would she lower down onto him, and then push hard.

She'd bite on his luscious lip. He'd beg for mercy. She'd ride him like a bitch and he'd love it. And just as he was about to come she'd pull almost completely off him and tease his tip.

She'd drive him wild with desire until finally she gave in, and slip him all the way into her, up to his hilt. He'd rock his hips, trying to get more. She'd rock hers in response. She'd go up and down his shaft, feeling him fill her.

They'd both become frantic, clutching onto each other's bodies, leaving traces of their scratching nails as they climbed higher.

Michael could see those beautiful eyes welling with tears as her walls came crumbling down, and she gave herself to him. She would be amazing. That beautiful body he knew she had would be tight against him, writhing in pleasure. She would come screaming his name. He could almost hear her now.

"Michael," she'd scream as they came together.

She had actually just screamed out his name as she climaxed alone. But weirdly she could almost hear him call out her name.

"Amanda," he cried out as he let himself go after she came for him, crying out for him, making him cry out for her.

Had he just said that out loud? He was certainly covered in his own excitement. He headed into the shower to clean himself off.

Visions of her were still whirring through his mind though. Great, he wanted her even more now. And there was no way she wanted anything to do with him. What a sap. He really needed to get a grip, and not in the way he just had.

Amanda headed into the bathroom, hoping a quick shower would clear her head. Did she really just fantasise about that blonde oaf? After the way he'd spoken to her? After the way he'd saved her life, actually.

After he'd offered her that bottle of water for her sick friend. After he'd smiled that beautiful smile. Wow; she'd been really ungrateful. The poor guy.

He'd gotten the rough side of her tongue on both occasions, when he'd actually been really nice to her. She felt so ashamed of herself as she realised what a bitch she'd been. And why?

Because somewhere along the line, when she was trying to be Miss Independent, she'd forgotten about love. She had grown afraid of commitment. And now here she was, fantasising about a guy she barely knew, but who had stirred up some very scary, but very real emotions.

As she padded back to her bed she saw the piece of paper scrunched up on her bedside table. She uncurled it, and tapped the number into her phone. She wrote out a text.

"Hi. I'm so sorry. I have no excuse for being such a bitch to you. I just didn't want to let you go without you knowing how grateful I really am. So, thank you. xx Amanda."

Michael was turning over on his bed again, not being able to get comfortable, when he heard his phone beep.

He was glad he was already lying down when he read the humble text. What could he say to that?

"You're welcome,' he started typing back. Umm…

"You can make it up to me over breakfast tomorrow."

Maybe she'd still feel overwhelmed though.

He quickly added, "You can bring Claire too if you want."

He hit send before he had a chance to back out.

"I'm a big girl. I'll brave it on my own. Where do you want to meet?"

He texted back a time and the name of a café in the town centre (that's the way her taxi had headed, so he hoped it was near her hotel).

He was careful to finish with a question mark. He was offering a suggestion, not making a demand. Wow; he was seriously paranoid. But he didn't want to mess up again.

Amanda replied with her assent, and was smiling as she leaned back down on her bed, eyes facing the ceiling.

'This is it, Trueman. Try to reign in your curt words. Just try to be nice to the guy that saved your arse. It's only breakfast; it doesn't mean you have to marry him. Just be polite.'

After a while, she managed to fall gently asleep, ensuring she'd set her alarm first. Michael was likewise finding slumber in spite of the butterflies trying to escape his stomach.

In the morning, Amanda had a refreshing shower and rummaged in her suitcase to find a suitable outfit.

She decided on the cotton tea dress she'd brought just in case they needed to look civilised in case of sightseeing. Dark green, and almost knee length, she felt it was respectable enough. The cap sleeves and v-neckline meant it was modest with a sexy air. Perfect.

She applied just a little makeup to hide any dark circles and to make her look more awake than she felt. A quick flick with the brush through her hair sufficed. Right; ready.

She slipped a note under Claire's door, so her friend would know where she was (if she woke up by the time she returned).

Deep breath in, and she started her walk around the corner. The café Michael had suggested was really close. She hoped he hadn't actually stalked her. Well, she'd just be on her guard. After last night's attack, being on her guard wasn't really an option; it was automatic.

She took big confident strides, trying not to make herself look like a target. She'd be damned if one arsehole would make her live in fear. She could walk down the street on her own in broad daylight. Yep, not nervous at all.

Still, she breathed out a long breath she hadn't realised she'd been holding as she rounded the corner and saw the blonde bombshell sitting at an outside table.

He got up as she approached (very *gallant*, and not patronising to her equal rights she reminded herself). He leaned in and kissed both her cheeks (very continental).

"Good morning, Amanda. I'm pleased you could make it. How are you feeling?"

"Morning. I'm good thanks."

"Is this table OK? We can go inside if you prefer?"

She took her seat opposite him as she replied, "This is fine."

Her heart was in her throat. She wasn't sure what to say (for once). But he was quiet himself. He passed her a menu in silence. Well, this was going well.

Michael went up to the counter and placed their order of croissants, orange juice and coffee. As he walked back to the table Amanda took note of the stonewashed jeans and tight white T-shirt he was sporting.

He hadn't looked that muscly under his long sleeved shirts, but woo, how gorgeously toned was he? Yum. Not overly done, just slender with great toning.

"Umm...I'm sorry. I didn't mean to make you think I was stalking you, Amanda."

"Please. I'm sorry I said it. I'm glad you were there. I don't know what I would have done without you. You were like a guardian angel. Thank you."

Michael's smile was one of slight embarrassment as she thanked him.

"You didn't get fired did you?" she asked, suddenly concerned.

"No. I'm not fired. Boss boy was a little pissed off, but he was OK once he got back in the club."

"Phew. So, was that who was chucking up that night?"

"Yeah."

"I thought you were just mates."

"Ha. That's the idea; inconspicuous protection. But no, he would never be my friend."

"Why?"

"Spoiled little rich boy? Not really friend material. Now, Henchman Number 1…"

Amanda blushed, "Did I really call him that?"

"Afraid so. But Mark is a good mate, the kind that will always have your back."

"Yeah. Claire's like that for me too. Only, we don't usually have to back watch quite like you do. You're a security guard, right?"

"I think minder is probably closer to it, but yeah, I'm a bodyguard. What do you do?"

There was a pause as their breakfast was put on their table, and Amanda took a welcome bite of croissant.

"Me? I'm just a dull admin."

"Now, that's not true. You may work in admin but you are certainly *not* dull."

"Well, my job is dull, but it does pay my bills. And yeah, at weekends I like to let my hair down and party."

"At least you get proper weekends. I seem to be forever working. Sure, I have the odd day off, but it's not what you'd call a weekend."

"That doesn't sound fun."

"I run my own company, so I'm never truly off duty. It's nothing grand, I don't have loads of staff, or anything. It's only a select few really."

"Kind of cool though."

"Believe me, it's not that glamorous. It's a lot of hard work. But then I do get some good assignments."

He prattled on, telling her about super yachts and the high life he was a voyeur of. He was always careful not to mention names though, of course.

As they finished their coffee, there was an awkward pause.

"Well, this was the nicest breakfast I've had for a long time," Michael commented.

"Mmm…yes, the coffee here is really good."

Michael grinned sheepishly.

"I was thinking more about the company," he said looking at her out of the corner of his eye, his head lowered so his fringe fell forward, his white teeth showing through his smiling lips.

"Oh. Yeah, it was really nice."

"So what now?"

"Now?"

"Yeah. Do we say goodbye? Or do you want to wander down by the marina?"

Amanda realised that she wasn't ready to say goodbye.

"Walk, please."

He proffered his arm so she could hold onto it as they got up to leave the café. After only a brief moment of hesitation, Amanda took hold of his fabulous forearm. It was all she could do not to snuggle in tight.

As they started walking she had to comment, "Oh Michael; what big muscles you have." (imitating the Little Red Riding Hood/Wolf moment).

"All the better to dance with you with."

"Dance?"

His Russian accent became exaggerated, "Michael Alkaev; ballet dancer extraordinaire."

And he did a quick pirouette right there in the street, making Amanda giggle. When did she become the simpering, giggling type? But she let the thought go as she marvelled at the exquisite spin.

"That is so cliché."

"I know, but my father was quite a traditionalist, and my mother liked the idea, so practically as soon as I could walk they started to shove me into ballet lessons. When we moved to the UK I was the only boy in the class. The girls teased me at first, but the teacher loved having a boy to teach. And as they started pointe work the girls were delighted to have someone to do promenades with."

"But you didn't make a career out of it?"

Now it was his turn to laugh.

"No. I wasn't really good enough, and it really doesn't pay well. I think my parents would have been OK with it, but no. I enjoyed it though. There's something so expressive and freeing in the movements."

"Well, you'll have to give me a command performance some time."

Amanda was still smiling.

"Any time you wish, but only for you."

He perked up as he realised she was talking about a time in the future.

"It does explain your gait though."

"Pardon me?"

"The way you walk; it's sort of lean and confident, with a kind of swagger."

He looked embarrassed again.

"Sorry. I wasn't supposed to notice that, huh?"

"It's just I'm not used to people looking at me. I'm usually the one doing the observing. Not necessarily a bad thing. I think I like you looking at me."

This was nice, Amanda thought as they continued to stroll. This was really nice. She felt so safe with him, not that she needed protecting, but it was nice all the same.

"Do you ever look just straight in front of you," she asked.

"Sorry?"

"You have a way of looking all around you with your eyes."

He halted and took her hands in his, bringing her to stand right in front of him.

"Maybe I could learn to," he whispered as he looked her straight in her eyes.

Her heart skipped a beat as she gazed into those dazzling sapphire depths. Their faces drew closer, so they were almost touching. She thought he was going to kiss her, but he turned away.

"Are you OK?"

"Yes. Sorry. I just…I don't know."

She pulled him back to her, and gave him no choice. She kissed him. It was tentative at first, searching, seeking, testing. His lips were full and soft. Her hand brushed his lightly stubbled cheek.

She stopped long enough to look into those baby blues to check this was OK. All she saw was wonder, heat and longing. She let her hand keep travelling round to the back of his head, her other hand falling to his firm waist.

She felt his hand cupping her face, as they both deepened the kiss, their tongues interlocking in their own private pirouette. She pulled in tighter, as flames shot through her core, igniting her soul.

She suddenly remembered they were out on the street just as she was about to moan in pleasure. She stopped. She looked at him, trying to catch her breath.

"Sorry."

"Do not apologise for that. That was…Amanda, you make me feel things I have never felt. I'm sorry. You probably don't want me to get mushy."

"I…I…think it's OK. I think you can be mushy. Honestly? I've not felt that alive in years. It's like you've woken part of me up that I didn't know was sleeping. I'm sorry. This isn't exactly first date stuff. And I'm not even sure I'm making sense."

"Maybe if we had longer we'd be more reserved?"

"Maybe if we had longer I would still be too afraid to do this at all," she murmured under her breath.

They were both quietly reflective as they wandered down to the marina. They found somewhere to sit down in the shade.

"Come closer," Michael muttered.

As she edged along he gently pulled her legs so they ended up across his lap, allowing him to gather her into his arms, enveloping her.

"I think all you really need is some TLC."

He didn't kiss her. He just held her. Amanda's head leaned against his chest. They didn't say anything. They didn't move. He just sat there, holding her safe in his embrace.

They sat there like that for ages. He could feel her slowly let go of her tension. It wasn't until he felt her shudder that he moved, and only then it was to delicately lift her chin.

There were salty rivers flowing down her cheeks which he wiped away with his thumb as best he could. He held on tighter, and kissed the top of her head.

"Shhh...I've got you," he said softly.

He started stroking her hair, which calmed her immediately.

"I'm...sorry...I...never...cry..." she sobbed.

"Shhh...it's OK," was the only response she got.

He just let her cry herself out. She pulled herself together, and found his hand gently wiping the remnants of her tears away from her face.

"Do you want to talk about it?" Michael asked her tenderly.

"Not much to tell really. Stereotypical bastard rat hurt me once upon a time."

"Ahh…Rattus Spurius. So, what happened?"

"I caught the love of my life in bed with another girl. Nothing happened except my heart got broken. I've spent the rest of my life aiming to have a good time. And I've succeeded. I vowed not to be the one to get hurt again."

"So why the tears?"

"I don't know. I've just not felt that kind of love again since."

"But you have now?

"Pah, love. I don't even know you. How can I possibly love you?"

"You never heard of *coup de foudre*?"

"Err…no."

"Love at first sight."

"Oh, I've heard tell of such things. But it usually involves a glass slipper, or some dwarves, or something."

"Well you see, usually I'd agree with you. But…in this case? But maybe it's not first sight."

"I think I would have remembered if I'd seen you before."

"Would you? What if it was in a former life?"

"A former life? You believe in that stuff?"

"Yes, especially now; it feels like I've known you all my life. See how you fit in my lap so perfectly? Do you sense how right it feels?"

"Yeah. You know what? I do. It's like it's meant to be. Ooh…how can I be talking such drivel? Really."

But she had to admit to herself it did feel very very nice.

"I just wish I had better answers for us. I'm working most of the rest of this week, and then you'll be jetting off home, leaving me here on my own to babysit still."

"If we don't have tomorrow, we had better make the most of today."

Just then Amanda's phone beeped. Shit, she'd forgotten she'd left Claire on her own. Her friend had only texted to check she was OK, but she was probably still feeling the aftershocks of last night.

"Let's get you back to your hotel," Michael offered kindly.

"Sorry. Today may be a bit tame after all."

They soon found a taxi and made their way back at the hotel where the girls were staying. Amanda shoved Michael into her own room as she went to check on Claire (who she knew wouldn't be dressed yet).

True to form, Claire had only just woken up when she sent the text, so was still plodding around in a towel, having just gotten out of the shower.

"How you feeling this morning?" Amanda asked.

"Fuzzy. You?"

"Good, actually. Michael came back with me. I met him for breakfast. You get my note?"

"Yes."

"Well, we went for a walk after, and he insisted on accompanying me to check that you're OK."

"Well, I'm fine. Don't let me get in your way."

"Just put some clothes on, and come to my room, OK?"

"I'm not up for a threesome."

"Eww, no. We won't be doing anything. Just come and say hi."

"I suddenly feel like your mum, offering approval."

"Just get up and get ready."

"Fine," Claire huffed resignedly.

Amanda dashed back to her room, where Michael was looking out the window to the balcony.

"Is it all secure?" she teased.

"Well, at least you locked the door," he smirked, "But I didn't like the look of the guy in reception."

"Ha ha. So, what do I do with you the rest of the day?"

"If you have to ask…?"

His lustful look could melt ice cubes. He pulled her close for a smooch. Oh, that tongue of his. What was she going to do? This was insane; they had no future together. She wasn't stupid. She knew how his life worked, even from the little he'd told her.

He was like the Littlest Hobo incarnate; wandering from place to place, helping the next poor soul who needed his protection. Where could she possibly fit into that? Damn the fates.

Why, when she'd finally let her guard down, and found a guy who pushed her buttons, why, did he have to be unobtainable? This was only going to lead to more pain. But, armed with that knowledge she could at least enjoy the precious little time she had with him.

A knock at her door broke her contemplation. She walked over to open it. She heard a cough behind her as she was about to just open it. She poked her tongue out at Michael, as she then made a show of looking through the spyhole in the door.

"Oh look; some evil bandit has come and politely knocked on my door. Oh no; wait, it's just Claire."

And she opened the door to admit her friend.

"Hi again," Claire was the first to speak.

"Hi, are you OK?" Michael asked with genuine concern.

"Yeah. Why does everyone keep asking me that?"

"Oh, I don't know; maybe because you had a terrible experience last night?"

"That might do it. Thanks by the way. I'm not sure if I said it last night in all the confusion."

"No worries. Have you plans for today?"

"Drinking a lot, and maybe finding some ibuprofen?"

"Oh dear. Hangover?"

"Yeah, your girlfriend and I polished off the vodka last night to calm our nerves."

Claire felt a jab in her ribs.

Quickly wiping the smirk off his face as he noticed the nudge, Michael asked, "Have you some swimming stuff?"

"Well der," Amanda mocked.

"Hem...well, would you like to put it on under some respectable clothes and join me in my hotel? I have ibuprofen, Alka Seltzer, and I'm sure they'll rustle you up a bacon sandwich."

"Sure. OK," Claire replied for them both, and went back to her room to change out of the clothes she'd only just put on.

"I just need to make a quick phone call," Michael said.

Amanda pointed to the balcony, and out he went, leaving her to get changed too.

When she came back out of the bathroom Michael was perched on the edge of her bed. She put a knee either side of his thighs, and sat facing him.

"Is this OK?" She was wearing the same dress, but he could now see a bikini strap poking out.

"It's more than OK," he breathed.

She ran her fingers through his hair, and he kissed her thoroughly once more. His hands reached round to her butt automatically.

"You sure we're OK to go in your hotel? I don't want you to get fired."

"That's why I called ahead. Hugo's alarmingly OK with it. Probably because he thinks he might be in with a chance with Claire."

"Nooo."

"Well, he remembered her from that night we met. Not sure how he remembered anything considering the amount he'd drunk, but he did."

"Well, I'm not sure Claire will feel the same about him. And if he's around, won't it be more like you're working?"

"I have a beautiful distraction today. I'll leave it up to Mark to keep tabs. I think I can trust the two of you not to be spies."

"How can you be so sure, Mr Bond?" she said trying out her best 'evil villain' Russian accent.

"Becaush my dear, you are more Mish Money Penny," he said with his best Sean Connery impression, making Amanda laugh.

Not being able to have sex with him was getting excruciating though. If it weren't for Claire she'd be shagging him right now. She couldn't remember the last time she'd not had instant gratification.

As the taxi pulled up outside, it was obvious this hotel was much grander than the one they'd just come from. This was confirmed by the wall-to-wall white marble as they wandered into reception. You could almost smell the money.

Michael took them up to his own room, where he pulled out a large bottle of water from the fridge, and 'plink plink fizzed' the Alka Seltzer. He handed the glass to a grateful Claire who was sitting on the white leather couch. He also cracked open the blister pack, and dropped two ibuprofen tablets in her hand, and poured a fresh glass of water.

"I like him," Claire stage whispered to Amanda.

"He's alright. He has his uses."

She just got a raised eyebrow from Michael's glimmering, amused eyes.

He disappeared into the bathroom to get changed himself.

Amanda was scoping out the room when he returned; it was really plush and very white. She smiled at the site of Michael in khaki shorts and a dark polo shirt, polished off with what could only be called deck shoes and wraparounds perched on top of his head. It seemed incongruous somehow.

He suddenly looked like a millionaire playboy (still stunning though). His tan only highlighted his magnificently sculptured muscles and cheekbones. Those calves that were now on show were definitely dancers legs; pure raw power harnessed and finely tuned. He'd obviously taken his dancing more seriously than he was prepared to admit.

"Better?" he asked Claire, ignoring Amanda's scrutiny.

"Getting there, thanks. Sorry to be a nuisance."

"Not at all. I like taking care of people. Now, do you want that bacon sandwich?"

"Mmm, yes please."

"Are you up to going downstairs, or would you prefer it here?"

"Downstairs will be fine. Thanks."

Down in the restaurant Claire wished she'd opted for room service. She felt a bit overawed by the décor, and underdressed for the occasion.

"You're fine," Michael whispered.

Had it been that obvious?

"Sorry. Reading people's part of the job description too," he offered.

"Is reading minds?"

"No, just body language."

She smiled nervously as she realised she'd just asked him that out loud. She felt a strong hand grip hers carefully and he lightly shook it.

"Relax," he told her.

And actually, she did. He shook her hand free, and she actually managed a smile as they were directed to a table.

"*Should I put this on your bill, sir?*" the waiter asked in Catalan, knowing full well the two young ladies weren't guests at the hotel.

"*Yes please, Jorge.*" Michael replied pronouncing the Spanish name beautifully, and pulling out the chair for Amanda.

Jorge was doing likewise for Claire. He left them menus, and disappeared discreetly.

"There's no bacon sandwiches on here," whispered Claire.

"It's OK. Jorge will get you one. Would you like an egg in it?"

"Just bacon please. I think I'll struggle eating it delicately as it is."

"And what would Amanda like to eat?"

"Just a salad for me, please."

When their lunch arrived there were two plates of bacon and egg sandwiches, and one exquisite salad. Michael winked at Claire as he picked up his sandwich and let the egg splurgle out and dribble down his chin.

Claire immediately relaxed and imitated her uncouth chaperone.

"Ahhh, that hit the spot," Claire announced, as she drank her second cup of tea.

"Thanks, Mikey."

He looked down at his phone as he accepted the thanks.

"Right, are you ready girls?"

"Yes," chimed the girls in unison.

Leaving a generous tip on the table for Jorge, the three walked out of the restaurant, out of the back door to the hotel, and down a path.

Chapter 4

"Isn't the pool down there?" Amanda asked, pointing in another direction.

"Who said anything about a pool? There's barely enough room for a goldfish in that thing."

"So where are you taking us?"

"This way."

He carried on leading them down the path, and across a beach, down to a jetty where the hotel's private boat was moored.

"Oh my god," Claire and Amanda exclaimed with a slight squeal.

"Afternoon ladies. Twenty-nine," Mark said as he welcomed them aboard.

"Twenty-nine?" Amanda queried.

"Ahem. This way ladies."

Michael steered them into the salon area where Hugo was waiting with welcome drinks. He shot Mark a look that could kill as he passed him.

"Hello ladies. Please make yourselves at home."

Hugo's Russian accent was definitely more pronounced than Michael's. He was slightly shorter, and of a slighter build. He was still athletic, but lacked the high toned definition in his muscles. His hair was a darker blonde, and his blue eyes were paler. He was good looking nonetheless, and certainly not scrawny.

The girls each took a glass of Champagne from the silver tray as directed, and said their hellos to their host. Amanda was a little surprised, knowing that Michael wouldn't choose to be friends with this guy, yet he was volunteering to share a boat with him on his day off.

"Amanda. Let me show you around."

Michael was at her side. She nodded and let herself be led out onto the deck. The hired skipper was just casting off from the dock.

"I'm so sorry. It was the best I could do at short notice. Hugo's OK. He's actually quite nice when he's sober, and he had the ability of hiring the boat. The hotel pool really is small, and there's more chance of us spending some time alone here. We're just going round the coast a bit to a quiet cove. We can ditch him there if you want."

Amanda put a finger up to his pert lips.

"Shhh…it's lovely."

She gave him a quick kiss, just so there was no doubt of her sincerity, of course.

He led her back inside, and showed her the other rooms. Yep; there was an en-suite bedroom they could use (handy). She thought she heard that this was a Sunseeker something or other. It was sleek and gorgeous whatever it was.

Claire and Hugo had ventured to the outside seating area where they joined them. They were well underway now, and the boat's motion had become steadier. They chatted freely and sipped Champagne as the boat made its way round to the cove.

The girls stripped to their bikinis and applied sun lotion to each other's backs (much to the wry amusement of the blokes), and teetered round to the front of the boat so they could sit on the big padded cushion. They felt like they were in one of those glossy magazine adverts.

It really was lovely; sun beating down, warming their skin. The cool sea breeze whooshed over them. It was in a word; luxurious.

They reached the cove much quicker than they would have wanted. Michael helped Amanda to her feet, and led her to the back of the boat.

He explained Mark was going to take the other two to shore with the skipper, giving them their much desired private space. Claire seemed happy enough with Hugo, so she agreed it was the best solution.

She hugged her friend before Claire precariously boarded the dinghy.

"Alone at last," Michael exclaimed, drawing Amanda close, looking at her lasciviously.

Just holding her like this was his luxury. He breathed in deeply as he revelled in this moment, this one precious moment that may well have to last him the rest of his days. He tried to put the idea to the back of his mind.

No thinking of tomorrow; if today was all they had he wanted to enjoy it without any shadows. He had a feeling Amanda felt the same way as she relaxed into his arms.

He looked down into those bright hazel eyes that made her seem so lost. He gave her a peck, which brought her smile out. How he loved that smile.

He gripped her hand and led her inside, through the lounge and through to the forward state room. He let his hands grope their way down her sides, past her bikini, feeling the naked flesh at her waist.

His breath hissed through his teeth as he breathed in, electricity sparking deep inside him. His erection was pleading to be set free from his shorts. He pulled her close to him, his hands on her lower back.

She grabbed his polo shirt and pulled it off him, finally revealing the fine pecs she'd suspected were there all along. She let her hands explore them, and glided around and down to his lower back and back up to his shoulders, anchoring herself as she looked up and found his mouth on hers, delving deep.

One of his hands went to the side of her head, all the time deepening their embrace. His fingers dragged through her hair, tousling it. He forced his head away from hers so he could tell her how beautiful she was, and how much he wanted to be inside her.

"I want you too," she murmured huskily.

She reached round her own back so she could undo her bikini top, and let it fall onto the deep piled carpet.

Her breasts pressed into his firm chest, skin on skin. The sensation sent shivers through the pair of them, and once more they began their desperate kiss, needing each other with greater passion with every passing minute.

Continuing with pecking kisses and panting breaths she reached down to his shorts to unbutton them, and those too were dropped to the floor.

His erection was now standing proud between them, and Amanda was impressed. But she longed to take him inside of her, wanted to feel that erection in her, needed him like she'd needed no other.

She pulled her bikini bottoms off and crawled onto the bed, giving him the best view as she did so.

"Oh Amanda," was all he could utter as he saw her other smile, which was just as beautiful as the one on her face.

She laid on her side, looking at him as he fumbled for his shorts pocket (where he'd put his condoms). She beckoned him close so she had the pleasure of rolling it on him. The sex was nothing like either had fantasised about; it was so much more.

She still insisted on being on top, but it lacked all the fury she had thought she felt. As soon as she mounted him she had a mini orgasm; overcome with the intensity that she felt.

His eyes rolled back in his head as he too was almost overpowered with sensation and emotion, combining together to form a concoction which felt almost lethal. He was panting with desire.

Beads of sweat had started trickling down between Amanda's breasts as she started pumping his cock, not with vehemence, but with deep all-encompassing strokes, wanting to draw this moment out. She leaned down and kissed him before adjusting herself so she could move faster.

The need in her was growing; she needed to feel him more. This exquisite ecstasy was almost too much to bear. She rocked her hips faster, and he was ready to match her pace, thrusting as much as he could. This was so much better than he could have hoped for; so much more intense.

Higher and higher they climbed, until at last they reached their peak together, their orgasm shattering everything in its wake, making them both cry out each other's names as they had once before when they'd been alone.

She collapsed down onto him, her head on his chest, his arms enveloping her. Her breaths were deep and laboured.

She felt a hand stroke her hair. Neither could find words for a long time. They just lied there, holding onto one another, revelling in the aftermath of their love making. Not fucking; actual love making.

This had reached into their very souls and united them deeper and with more meaning than anything else ever could.

Eventually Amanda rolled off and onto her back next to her lover. He pulled himself up so he could look down on her, absorbing her beauty.

"Thank you," he whispered.

It was all he could say. In that one solitary act she had given him all she could give him, as he had given his all to her. His hand brushed her cheek as he softly kissed her lips.

Reluctantly, they had to get up off the bed eventually. They pulled on their beachwear and wandered out onto the deck. They could see the shore from here.

"How well can you swim?" Michael asked.

"Well enough to get to there," she said proudly, nodding towards the beach.

She didn't like to confess to having won medals at college level. With a beautiful swan dive, Michael dived into the beautiful turquoise sea. Amanda watched as a pair of angel wings appeared before her eyes.

How had she not noticed that tattoo before? Well, she'd not exactly been looking at his back, had she? It was beautiful; intricate but not overbearing.

As he trod water Michael looked back towards the boat to see Amanda dive in with grace. When she surfaced it was right up close to him. She was beaming.

They both headed for the shore together. The water was refreshing after their earlier exertions.

They walked out of the sea and up to the beach hand in hand. Mark was on hand with towels, cool lemonade and Pringles. To Amanda's surprise, Hugo was smooching her friend a little further up the beach. She turned her back to give them their privacy.

"Any lotion in your bag of tricks, Number Two?" Michael asked Mark.

"Aye aye, Twenty-nine," was his response as he tossed him a bottle.

"OK. Number Two has got to be some saddo Trekkie reference," Amanda observed.

"But I'm still stumped by the Twenty-nine. It's not your age, is it?"

"First turn over, I want to get this stuff on your back before you burn."

She rolled her eyes, but complied. As he rubbed lotion onto her back tenderly he provided an explanation, once again emphasising his Russian accent (she loved it when he did that).

"You ever hear of the MIG 29? It's a Russian jet fighter aircraft. Mark thinks it's funny because I was born in Russia like the MIG. And also, MIG sounds like Mick. Ha ha ha."

His teeth pulled back in a sarcastic smile at Mark.

"Yeah, and because you're just as deadly," chipped in Mark.

"And what's so sad about Star Trek?" he added.

Amanda fake coughed, "Geek!"

She rolled over onto her back.

"Ahh. But you knew. You knew it was a TNG reference."

She smiled at Mark.

"OK. You got me. Live long and prosper."

She held up her hands with her fingers held in pairs, imitating the Vulcan sign of peace. He smiled back before returning to his watch over the beach.

Although, they were pretty secluded here, so they were as safe as they could be. And the boat wasn't going anywhere as the skipper was making the most of some sneaky R&R time on the beach with them.

Michael's hands had turned their attention to Amanda's front, ensuring there wasn't a square inch not protected from the sun. He kissed her when he'd finished, leaving her to bask in the sun like a (very beautiful) lizard.

He quickly smothered some lotion onto himself too, just to prove he was a good boy. They just lay there soaking up the rays together, holding hands. They were both enjoying some proper relaxation at long last. It felt like aeons since either of them had felt truly relaxed like this.

Having rested long enough, Amanda having realised she didn't really know anything about Michael decided it was time to ask something akin to twenty questions.

"So, how are old are you, Twenty-nine?"

"Actually, it's pretty close. I'm thirty."

"Shock, gasp, so old."

"Come off it. OK, your turn."

"Twenty-six."

"Ahh; so young?"

"Yeah, alright. Ummm... where do you live?"

"Nowhere and everywhere."

"What; you don't have a house anywhere that you can call home?"

"No. My folks live in Shropshire these days. Does that count?"

"OK. Close enough. Kind of sad though."

"Just nomadic. I wanted to see the world."

"Have you seen enough of it yet?"

"Enough to know you're the most beautiful girl in it."

"Smoothy!"

"Sorry. Was a bit cheesy, eh? But you really are gorgeous. How many boyfriends have you had?"

"Two. King Rat and now you. And yourself?"

"Three, I guess. If we're counting us. Different from sexual partners though."

"Yeah. Not going there."

"Yeah. Maybe not. So, did you go university?"

"Yeah, I did my degree at Manchester Uni. It was a good idea at the time, but it's got me an admin job so far. Wahoo. Did you go?"

"University? Yes. I did my degree in Modern Languages. I just wanted to spend a year in a foreign country really."

"What, England didn't count?"

"Well, we moved there when I was so young, and I have dual nationality, so no. England doesn't count, as it is my home."

"Oooo…touched a nerve. Sorry."

He leaned on his side, propping himself up on his elbow to look at her, whilst his free hand smoothed her hair.

"What I really want to know is…how did you get so beautiful?"

"Genetics," she winked.

He moved in for a kiss.

"Get a room you two."

Claire was bounding up to meet them.

"Hi hunny. You OK? You two have been huddled away over there for ages."

"Yeah, I'm good. Hugo's really sweet when you get to know him."

"Please, I don't need to hear this," Michael protested.

"Sorry. Yeah, bit weird for you. Anyway, we were going to head back to the boat, are you ready to join us?"

"You sure you don't want some alone time first?" Amanda asked.

"No. We're not all rampant, you know."

Michael got up to help Mark pack the stuff up.

"So, what's he like?" Claire asked as soon as they were alone.

"Oh…my…god."

She fanned herself in her impression of Janice from Friends.

"Claire; I think I'm in trouble."

"What? He got you pregnant already?"

"Ha ha. No. I think we said the 'L' word already, and I think I meant it."

"Love?" Claire gasped.

"I know. I know. But it's awful. Claire, we have no future. He's a bodyguard. I've seen the film; it doesn't end well for Whitney in that."

"Shit. I hadn't thought about it, but yeah. I guess he's all over the place."

"Place? World. He travels the whole *world* with his job. It's what he loves, and I'd never ask him to give it up for me. It's a mess."

"Oh, I'm so sorry."

"Hey, your uber rich guy's the same too. What, like we're ever going to see either one of them again after this week?"

"No. I guess not. But it's exciting as far as holiday romances go. I thought it was just going to be anonymous sex, but no. You bagged a bodyguard, and I got a billionaire's son. Not too shabby."

"I'm trying to enjoy it whilst I can. Just help me next week, OK?"

"Next week and always, babe."

They all boarded the dinghy, and headed back to the yacht. The sun was starting to go down. The skipper got the blankets out for the girls before heading back to the dock. They huddled up in the saloon with yet more Champagne, the guys on either side of them.

Hugo had really shown his humble bashful side today, and now was no exception.

"Claire. Umm…would you like to…err…would you have dinner with me tonight, please? You and Amanda? And Michael, of course."

It was so strange. He was so arrogant when he was out at the clubs. But here, relaxed and amongst friends you could clearly see his quiet reserve.

"Dinner sounds lovely, Hugo. Thank you. But, and I do hate to sound girly, we kind of have nothing to wear."

"Not a problem. We can stop by a shop on the way back and buy you girls outfits."

"That really is too generous."

"Pah. Let me do this, please. I get so few chances to get out and enjoy myself."

"OK. You win. You may buy me clothes, and feed me yummy food," Claire smiled at him.

Michael squirmed a little but said nothing. He clearly didn't approve, but couldn't voice his disapproval. Amanda started to appreciate why you shouldn't mingle socially with your boss.

She didn't quite feel comfortable with Hugo buying her an outfit either, but she could see it would just cause an argument if she tried to refuse. He wanted to do this. From what Michael had hinted at, Hugo was pretty much a prisoner in his own home. So, if he wanted to have some fun doing this, who was she to stop him?

As they walked down the jetty Mark was at the rear of the pack, and Michael was with Amanda at the front. He was combing the beach for any signs of trouble, clearly back on duty, but still trying to look casual about it. They went up to the rooms so they could all shower and change.

"Are you OK?" Amanda asked Michael when they were alone in his room.

"I'll be fine."

"Future tense? You don't want to go out to dinner, do you?"

"Not with him, no. I'll be on my guard, and not totally with you. This is supposed to be my day off. The boat trip? That was fine as I knew we'd be able to distance ourselves, but *dinner*? But what can I say? He's the boss."

"Come here."

Amanda linked her arms behind his lower back as she snuggled up close, offering comfort.

"Mmmm…that helps a little."

"What about this?"

She pecked his lips.

"A little more."

She bit down gently on his lower lip.

"OK. That helps a bit too much. We have to be quick."

"I can be quick."

She led him into the bathroom, and turned the shower tap on. She peeled off Michael's polo shirt and chucked it on the floor. Next his shorts were treated with equal disdain.

She wriggled out of her now wrinkled dress and her bikini. She nudged him into the now steaming shower, and let the water gently cascade over his tanned skin. It was soothing and erotic all at once.

She stepped in close behind him, letting their wet skin come into tantalising contact. She licked his neck, all the way up to his ear, gently biting his lobe. The pleased groan from him was her encouragement. She cupped the top of his shoulders with her hands and slowly massaged his deltoids with her thumbs, slowly increasing the pressure as she moved in big circles. His head fell back as he let out an 'aaahhh' of pleasure and relaxation.

She felt him relax under her thumbs, his shoulders slowly lowering. Her hands felt their way down to his angel wings, still easing his tension with her thumbs digging in under his shoulder blades.

She put some shower gel into her hands as she moved her hands round to his pecs. Her front was now in full contact with his gorgeously pert bottom. She soaped her way down his body, going as far as his navel before working her way back up. This earned her a little grown of frustration, which disappeared as she shampooed his hair.

Her fingers explored his cranium, running through his golden locks. He fell almost into a trance at her touch. She nibbled his neck as her hands ran back down south. This time they didn't stop. They brushed his erection with tingling pleasure. His breath caught as he hissed in.

She took him firmly in her hand and started massaging his cock. His head and shoulders leaned back on her, as he gave himself up to her control. The pouring water made her gliding action smooth and delectable.

She moved her hand a little faster and gripped a little firmer, his groans becoming moans as she did. She could feel the electricity of his lust spark through her, making her lean her hips into his butt. Her hand was moving fast now as she felt him approach his climax, his moans becoming louder and more urgent.

On she continued until he went over the edge and came then and there, under her control. He steadied himself with a hand on the shower wall before letting the water rush over his head to revive himself.

He turned to her, and kissed her passionately as the water washed over their bodies.

"Thank you again," he murmured as he in turn, shampooed her brunette waves.

His hands ran down her body as he washed her, but she wouldn't let him return the favour. This was his treat, and she'd keep it at that.

They quickly dried themselves off, and Amanda gazed down at her poor shambles of a dress. But it's all she had with her here, so she had no option but to put it back on, along with her still damp bikini as underwear. She hoped somehow they could buy a bra and knickers too, otherwise tonight could be a tad uncomfortable, and she wasn't going to go commando.

Chapter 5

Amanda was relieved to see Claire looking just as dishevelled as she felt in the hall as they reconvened. They just laughed at each other.

"You Worzel," Claire mocked, insinuating her friend looked like a scarecrow.

"Right back at ya."

"Oh no, this will never do. Definitely shopping time," Hugo said with mock disdain.

The hotel's private hire car was waiting for them out the front, but the girls felt really self-conscious climbing into such luxury looking like they'd been pulled through a hedge backwards.

The chauffeured car made its way through the town, Mark riding shotgun, with the double daters in the back.

They pulled up outside a boutique, Michael opening the door for the rest of them. Mark stayed by the car, looking dapper in his suit.

The shop assistant all but sneered at the girls, but Hugo paid no attention to her.

"I'm afraid our friends have spent too long on the beach today. They've not had time to go back to theirs to change. Do you have something they can wear to dinner, please?"

His Russian accent always commanded respect for some reason. The assistant snapped out of her bitch mode, and got busy rummaging through rails to look for something for the girls, and took them to the changing rooms out the back.

"Getting there," Hugo announced as they came back into the shop wearing two very glamorous gowns, and carrying carrier bags with their dishevelled clothes in.

He shoved his credit card across the counter, before walking them two shops down to buy some shoes.

They got back into the car and were driven to a hair dresser who was clearly on standby for them.

The girls had their hair styled as assistants gave them a quick manicure. This was polished off with a quick spritz of makeup.

The boys had disappeared whilst these preparations were taking place, but now walked back in with admiring smiles.

Hugo held out an open jewellery box to Claire. Michael spread out his hands in a resigned shrug behind Hugo's back, with an 'I couldn't stop him' expression.

Claire gasped as ruby and diamond earrings and a necklace which matched her red satin dress dazzled her.

"Just the icing on the very beautiful cake," Hugo drooled.

"And not forgetting the other pretty lady."

He passed a similar box to Amanda, but this one had emeralds inside.

"Hugo, this is just too much, I can't accept these."

"Please Amanda."

He took her to one side.

"Please. I may act like an ignorant idiot, but even I can see when my staff are happy. He has done so much for me, and I know he has to put up with a lot. Please let me do this for him, if not for you."

His whisper was full of admiration for Michael.

"OK. Thank you. But no more, OK? It just feels wrong. I can't see that Michael and I have a future past this week."

"No more, I promise. Just dinner. But no future?" he asked with concerned curiosity.

"We live in very different worlds, and neither of us can see how it could ever happen."

"This is indeed very sad."

"Promise me…I know this is wrong as he's paid to protect you…but will you look out for him, please?"

"You need not even ask."

"Thanks Hugo. Has anyone ever told you you're older than your years?"

"No. But I take the compliment. Thank you. Shall we…?" he said, gesturing with his hand that they should join the others.

They all got back in the car once more and drove out to the prestigious restaurant. It was dark and candlelit, with glasswear gleaming in the glow. Subtle music infused the atmosphere with a romantic ambience.

Of course, it made poor Mark's job a little harder in the dark, but he was seated where he had a good view of people entering and was yet still within eyesight of the two couples.

The foursome was seated with a spectacular view of the cove which was illuminated by moody lighting.

"You look radiant," Michael whispered to Amanda as they found their seats.

The emeralds and candlelight were making her hazel eyes shimmer all the more brilliantly.

He pulled out her chair for her as she sat down, before taking his place opposite her, and next to his boss (or at least the boss' son), and looking towards the door.

He was on edge already, scanning the other diners as they'd walked in, checking escape routes etc. This was such a bad idea.

He felt Amanda's foot nudge his under the table. He looked into her eyes and couldn't help but smile back, her smile was just infectious.

The food was delectable; simple yet ever so well done in a contemporary style. It looked almost too good to eat. And naturally, it was all washed down with more Champagne. The girls had already sipped on pre-dinner cocktails.

Despite himself, Michael managed to enjoy the evening, and became absorbed in the romantic atmosphere. But all night he was trying to think of a way to be with Amanda.

He couldn't imagine spending his life without her in it, but couldn't think of a way to include her in it. There had to be an answer. Never had he imagined he'd ever feel this way, and especially not in so short a time.

Shouldn't he know her before being this emotionally invested? But almost as soon as he'd seen her he'd known. And when he'd seen her kissing that guy in the club that first night it had taken unimaginable willpower not to go over and deck the guy; a jealous urge had consumed him, and he hadn't even spoken to her then.

There was an instant recognition, as if some higher force had willed them together. He also pondered when he'd become such a girl. Love at first sight? Destiny? Next he'd be arranging flowers.

"Michael?" Amanda's voice brought him back to Earth with a bump.

"Sorry?"

"Hugo was saying how much he was enjoying being able to do something normal. He was thanking you for allowing us all to do this."

"Sorry; I was lost in thought. But you're welcome. I'm just sorry you can't do it more often."

He began to wonder if the boy's father would start relaxing the lock and key routine now his son had proved he could be responsible, and that there weren't assassins hiding around every corner. But then Ibiza was a million miles away from where Hugo lived. It was just so sunny and tranquil here; it felt like paradise. Or was that Amanda's influence?

The four of them ate and drank and talked and laughed, but all too soon it was time to leave. None of them felt like a wild night of clubbing after such a civilised meal, so they headed outside to the car.

"Amanda; spend the night with me."

It was more of a plea than a request.

"Are you sure that's OK?"

"I'm technically still on my day off. It's OK. I'll be back on duty in the morning, but tonight is mine, and I want to share it with you. I want you to be in my arms in the morning; to be the first thing I see."

"Well, since you ask so nicely, Mr…errr…"

She didn't even know his surname? So much was still a mystery, and forever would be, she feared.

"Alkaev."

"Alk-eye-ev? OK. I can handle that, I think. What was I saying, Mr Alkaev?"

"You were saying yes, and making me very very happy," he breathed around a naughty smile as he reached up to smooth his thumb across her cheek.

He pressed his lips to hers briefly in a stolen kiss, before opening the car door for her.

It wasn't until they were about to go into his room that it dawned on Amanda that they hadn't dropped Claire off at their hotel. She'd been wrapped up in a big strong arm as she'd leaned into Michael in the car; it was kind of distracting.

She looked down the corridor and caught her friend's eye, and threw her a raised eyebrow of inquiry. But her friend was grinning at her and gave her on 'OK' wink.

Happy in the knowledge her friend was alright she turned back to Michael who was holding the door open for her with a very wicked grin of his own. He was in the doorway so she had to squeeze past him to get into the room.

"There are so many things I want to do to you," he whispered right into her ear, his warm breath firing through all her synapses, making her bite her lower lip in anticipation.

She took a couple of steps further into the room, but was halted by a sturdy arm grabbing her waist from behind. He turned her round to face him and caught her chin between his thumb and forefinger, and planted a kiss on her sweet sweet lips.

His voice was a low soft rumble as he murmured, "But…" (kiss) "first…" (kiss) "we need…" (kiss) "to get you" (kiss on the neck) "out of this…" (kiss on the shoulder) "silky soft" (a strap was lowered so he could kiss more of her shoulder) "dress".

She was his; utterly under his spell as he slowly bent down on his knees and kissed an ankle as he lifted her foot in his hands and removed first one shoe then the other. He gathered the hem of her gown in his hands and started raising it inch by slow blissful inch, placing tender kisses every step of the way.

As he got to her belly button he turned the kisses to little laps until he reached her breasts, which were mercifully naked with nipples that were just begging for his attention. He took one in his mouth and drew his head back ever so slowly and nipped his way over to the other nipple, repeating the lick and suck.

He raised her dress the rest of the way over her head, her hair falling with a bounce back around her shoulders.

She launched herself at him so she could get a proper tongue lashing snog, her leg raising up to his hip, trying to feel him with every part of her body, her hands grabbing on to his face, then tugging onto his hair, round to the back of his head, forcing him closer. The intensity of her need was overpowering her.

They both went for his shirt buttons, and ended up fumbling at them, so he grabbed hold and ripped his shirt off, almost screaming in pain as his lust increased.

His hands slanted down at her hips, and grasped onto her, their mouths colliding together. He fumbled down to his trousers, and with shaking hands threw them off him. As he did, she climbed out of her new silk knickers and threw herself onto the bed.

He lunged himself onto her, her legs widening to make way for his mass.

She was writhing, clasping onto his buttocks, urging him into her. She could feel her pussy pulsing red hot with desire. She needed him so badly.

His lips were biting their way up her neck, accompanied by groans.

"Ahh…Amanda…"

The bittersweet stabbing agony.

"Mi…chael," she cried in return.

With one fluid move he launched into her, their bodies twisting and merging. He was ramming himself into her, wanting to bury himself in her forever. Flames were licking through them and engulfing them, their muscles going taught with anticipation as they carried on driving onwards.

Their hands were frantically searching one another, trying to grab on, trying to cling on to this precious feeling, trying to reach out to their climax which was within their grasp already. Their mouths were crashing. Their desperation growing hotter still, scorching them.

Her hips were off the bed as she drove herself forward, welcoming the full force of his thrusts.

Sweat began beading down his brow, and his plump lips parted in a silent gasp, his eyes tightening but he didn't close them fully. He wanted to keep looking her in the eyes.

Amanda's back was arching, but still she kept her eyes locked on his, her teeth gritted.

Their gasps reached a crescendo as they both climaxed, bursting into a million pieces, their bodies pulsing.

They both cried out in unison, "I love you!"

He carried on his intense thrusts as he cried out his bliss along with her. Their bodies finally slowed, leaving empty shells trying to gasp in more air again.

He collapsed on the bed next to her, draping an arm across her, nipping her mouth with tiny kisses, which moved to more lingering ones.

Their eyes were glittering, and their grins grew wide at the realisation of what had just occurred; earth shattering joy.

They giggled, overcome with their happiness. His hand brushed her face.

"I really do love you, Amanda."

"And I love you, Mr Alkaev."

"Argh, what are we to do? I don't want this to end."

And just like that, their little bubble of happiness burst.

"I know. Me neither."

They just laid there hugging, holding on to the only thing that seemed to matter anymore. She turned around, so they were spooning. He nuzzled into her hair, breathing in her scent.

"Mmmm…you smell so good I just want to eat you," he leered, nipping into her neck.

She rolled around, giggling and protesting, pleading him to stop as he tickled her.

Breathless, she lay there on her back, looking up at him. He stroked her hair out of her eyes, and planted another kiss.

"We'll think of something," Mikhail murmured.

She turned on her side to face him.

"I hope so."

They hugged each other close, and just looked into one another's eyes until they finally closed in sleep, exhausted after their treasured day together.

The next morning Michael was up bright and early, ready for work.

Amanda was still asleep as his phone discreetly buzzed as a text was received.

He quickly but quietly (somewhat like a Ninja) went through the connecting door to Hugo's room. As he approached Hugo's bed he realised too late Claire was still there, and got an eyeful of her boobs. Now there was something he didn't need to see. Besides, Amanda's were much more gorgeous.

He quickly turned his back, and mumbled an apology.

"You wanted to see me, Hugo?"

"Yes. Today we're going to Can Marça Caves."

"Oh, we *are*, are we?"

"Excuse us, please."

The request to Claire was from Hugo. She quickly shoved on the hotel bathrobe.

"Can I go through there?" she asked Michael, pointing at the adjoining door.

"No. Amanda's still asleep. Just go out on the balcony, or something."

His reply was gruff. He was clearly not impressed.

Hugo waited for her to get out of earshot before speaking again (now in Russian).

"You didn't have to be so rude."

"Me? You drag me in here at an inappropriate moment, and start making demands. And I'm being rude? I thought you were in danger!"

"I was merely making my intention clear."

"Well, now it's clear. And as your security advisor, I'm making it clear that it's a really bad idea," Michael's voice was firm and hard, but not yet raised.

"You said you wished I could get out more."

"And I do. But do you understand the risks? The caves are remote, there is only one way in and out. There are many places for people to hide out of sight."

"Michael. You are starting to sound like my father. There are no boogie men. Danger is not at every turn. I just want to go to a tourist site. There will be lots of tourists. Nobody would try anything in such a public place. I want the girls to come with us."

"Claire fine. Amanda no. How can I protect you if I'm distracted?"

"We'll blend in more this way. Besides, I want you to enjoy yourself."

"I'm supposed to be working. Your father pays me to look after your welfare, not to have dates."

"I am not going to beg. I am going to the caves, and I am going to be like a normal human being. I cannot live with this paranoia any longer. How many times have you had to save my life in the time you've worked for me? None. You can either come with us and do your job, or I go on my own and you get fired."

Hugo's eyes were glowering a dare for Michael to argue any further.

"Fine, but if you get killed I want people to know it wasn't my fault. Mark won't be joining us. He needs a rest, he's not slept properly in days."

"Yes, I know. Mark has today off. Be ready in half an hour. I want breakfast first."

Michael strode back through to his room, slamming the door, waking up Amanda. He was so angry he wanted to punch something. Amanda was looking at him with wide eyes, all trace of sleep dissipating as she sensed his anger.

"Of all the stupid things. And making demands. *высокомерный сын сука!*"

He spat the words through clenched teeth, his fury firing out of his eyes as he called Hugo an arrogant son of a bitch behind his door, as he'd been unable to do so to his face.

Amanda had no idea what he'd said, but it didn't take a genius to know it wasn't good.

"Michael. What's happened?"

"Hugo wants to go to see the pretty lights in the caves."

This was laden with sarcasm and said through a snarl.

"I'm sorry. I don't understand."

"They're remote, and full of hiding places, and Mark has the day off. And he wants you girls to come too. I can't do this."

His look was now of pained concern.

"Shhhh…" she soothed, and slowly crept up to him.

She took his hand gently in hers.

"Breathe."

Her contact and soft voice had an instant calming effect on him. She let go of his hand and reached up to cup the back of his neck, and stroked with her thumb, then did the same behind his ear.

He looked at her curiously. She just kissed him in response. She took his hand again and led him to sit down on the bed.

"Now. Can you tell me why you suddenly can't protect him?"

"Because of you."

"Me? I think I'm sorry I asked."

"I didn't mean it in a bad way. But he wants us all to go out together again, only this time I have no backup and I can't be with you like I want to be. It won't be even like yesterday. I don't want to treat you this way. I don't want you to feel like you're less important than that shithead."

"Did it ever occur to you I may be able to help?"

"Help?"

"Yes. Ever hear that two heads are better than one? I can be an extra set of eyes."

"But."

"But nothing. If anything happens you will handle it."

"I can't protect all three of you. Amanda, I will be caught between the one I love and the one I'm supposed to protect because that's what I'm paid to do. I'd hesitate, and that could cost you both your lives."

He looked like he was in pain.

"OK. What's the real risk of anything bad happening?"

"OK. There's been no sign we were followed here. Despite his flamboyance, I've tried to keep him discreet. Apart from that mugger who was more interested in you, there's been no trouble. I hope we're safe, but I cannot assume that."

"OK. So, how about we go and see how it goes? If you get so much as a hunch of anything untoward we come back. Yes?"

"I couldn't bear it if you got hurt."

"And I won't. I'm a big girl, I can take care of myself."

"Based on the other night?"

"That's not fair. I was drunk and caught off guard. Part of the reason I got shitty at you was because I was embarrassed. I've had self defense training, and I used to do Taekwondo."

"Oh. Hmm. I can see how you'd be embarrassed. You really did Taekwondo?"

"Yes. My parents always wanted to be sure I could be safe. I'm not saying I'd get in and fight with you. I'm just saying if it came down to it I'd hold my own, and get away to safety. You protect Hugo; no hesitation, OK?"

"OK."

With Michael pacified, they got ready quickly.

"I have to stick with him whilst he goes to breakfast," Michael apologised.

"Claire and I need to go to our hotel to get changed anyway. Neither a rumpled dress nor an evening gown seems quite appropriate for walking around a cave. We'll grab a taxi somewhere."

"No. I'll get reception to call a taxi for you," he said, and quickly made the phone call.

They knocked and walked through into Hugo's room. Michael signed to Mark to go to his room to get some downtime.

Having been a silent witness to the argument he disappeared without saying a word, but he did pat Michael on the shoulder encouragingly as he went past him.

"The girls need to get changed. I'm getting a taxi called for them," Michael said matter-of-factly to Hugo.

"OK."

Hugo turned to Claire.

"Don't be long. I'll wait for you to get back, and we can all have breakfast together."

"It's OK," Amanda chipped in.

"We can get something at our hotel. It'll be quicker."

"Fine. But I'm not happy about it."

Amanda linked arms with Claire as they sauntered out of the room, waving behind them.

'Sometimes,' thought Amanda, 'Hugo is *not* older than his years.'

Chapter 6

"Can you wait here, please?" Amanda asked the taxi driver.

She thought Michael had already ordered a return trip, but it never hurt to make sure. And she didn't want to give him any more cause for concern. The driver nodded his agreement.

As the girls trotted up to their room Claire asked, "So, what was with all the Russian argument between the boys about?"

"Hugo didn't tell you?"

"No. He was just sullen when Michael stormed out so I got dressed and hid in the bathroom."

"Chicken!"

"No. Just sensible."

"Michael's not happy about today."

"Why?"

"Because he's back in his official role today, and not that of 'boyfriend to Amanda Trueman'. He's feeling the pressure of being bodyguard to him and trying not to totally neglect me."

"Oh."

"Yes oh. But to be honest, I'll take every minute I can get. Neglected or not."

"Carpe diem."

"Look at me; I'm seizing already."

Amanda did a heroic pose as she said this, making the pair giggle.

They threw on shorts and T-Shirts, and picked up day bags. They quickly popped into a shop and bought coffee and croissants which they ate in the car on the way back to the swanky hotel.

The boys were waiting for them on the comfy sofas in reception. They both looked like a pair of teenagers as they smiled nervously at their returning dates.

They all piled into the same taxi Claire and Amanda had just used. Michael had led the way outside, looking about him subtly, and taking the front seat in the car.

Hugo was sat between to the two girls, which he was happy with. He made them laugh a few times en route, and each time Michael's hackles bristled at the sound.

As they drove along Michael was seemingly chatting to the driver in Catalan. What he was actually saying was how he wanted the driver to drop them off but then park up out of sight, but not too far away.

He took the driver's number so he could call him when they were ready to return. He subtly took out a wad of cash and handed it to the driver as a down payment.

Michael was already scanning as the car pulled up. There were quite a few people milling around but nothing out of the ordinary. He opened the door on Amanda's side, who had sat behind him.

As they all started to walk away from the car Michael fell into step between Hugo and Amanda. He paid for the tickets, and huddled them together out of the way to wait for the next guided tour. He felt like a bloody sheepdog herding sheep. But hey, his Amanda was here. That had to be a good thing.

Eventually, they were all led into the caves. Michael held them back so they were at the rear of the group.

The guide told them about the fabulous stalactites and stalagmites as they wandered through. There were some amazing lighting effects, accompanied by music. It made the whole experience feel even more mystical. Even Michael had to confess his admiration, but he still felt like a cat on a hot tin roof.

There were shadows everywhere. But hang on, that shadow was moving the wrong way. Shit! He put himself in front of the group and backed up a little.

Voices were echoing all around them. He knew this had been a bad idea. Shit. Why had he let himself get talked into this?

Hugo rightly looked sheepish, whilst Amanda's heart was in her mouth as she glanced around them, trying to plan their escape route.

Just as they were about to make a run for it, from around the corner, came a child. Bloody stupid lighting casting large shadows.

They all took a deep breath, but nobody admonished Michael. The shadow had looked like an adult, and he'd only been doing his job.

They re-emerged forty minutes after they had made their entrance. Michael called the taxi back, and shepherded them all in. Safe in the car they began to relax again, and even managed to laugh about the 'monster child'.

Michael paid the driver the balance of the promised amount and some, as they arrived safely back at the hotel.

"So what do we do now?" Michael asked Hugo, just glad to be back in one piece.

"Well, after the scary shadow experience, I need a drink. Ladies?"

"God yes!"

So they all headed to the bar in the hotel. Yet more Champagne flowed. Michael only had a tiny sip of Amanda's though. He wanted something to steady his nerves, but refused to compromise his vigilance.

The more bubbly they drank the more the three relaxed. Hugo loved hearing about the way Claire and Amanda lived. To his inexperienced ears, going to an office and working in administration, helping people sounded fascinating.

He confessed to wanting to be an 'Average Joe'. He couldn't quite believe it when the girls explained it was really dull. But he did sympathise with the fact that they *had* to work. If he ever worked it would be for his father but at boardroom level, and only if he wanted to.

His father was more than happy keeping his son locked up in his ivory tower for the time being. When he was younger, Hugo's days had been filled with happiness, as his nannies lavished attention on him.

His mother had died in childbirth. Amanda thought how lonely his life sounded, and knew which life she'd choose. She may not be rich, but she was relatively happy, and mostly; she had her freedom.

It seemed Hugo had always been treated as a precious reminder of his mother. His father had been utterly devoted to her, and couldn't bear the thought of losing his son too. So, when the death threats started he'd reacted the only way he could; by hiding him away from the world.

"I think…" Hugo's voice was already a little slurred. "I need lunch. Care to join me?"

"No argument from me," Claire chimed enthusiastically.

He leaned in and kissed her in gratitude, before leading her into the restaurant.

"Table for four, sir?" the waiter enquired.

"Yes please," Hugo replied.

As he showed them to a table Amanda said quietly, "*Gracias, Jorge.*"

He smiled warmly at her, almost as much as Michael did.

"*De nada,*" was his polite reply as he handed out menus.

After having munched through another delicious lunch the group felt replete. Hugo whispered something into Claire's ear, making her chuckle and nod. He said something in Russian to Michael who gave a single nod of assent.

He led the way upstairs, and left Amanda in his own room whilst he went and double checked Hugo's before leaving him there with Claire. He went back into his own room, where Amanda was waiting with an expectant look.

"Sorry. Not now. *Hugo* may be getting busy, but me? I am still on alert."

He flashed her a pout.

"Huh. OK. So what do we do whilst we wait?"

"Well, normally I'd read."

"You want to read?"

He laughed awkwardly, "No. I said I normally read. Honestly, I'm not sure what to do now. I just know it can't be what I really really want to do. It's too early to interrupt Mark. He's been on 24/7 pretty much since we got here."

"So, ummmm...TV?" she suggested.

"Looks that way. There's a list of films to watch," he said as he passed her said list.

Amanda looked through the films and laughed.

"There's a film about you."

"Really?"

"Yeah. The Bodyguard. I can't believe it. How old is that?"

"Amanda."

"Yeah."

"I have to tell you something."

"What?"

Not liking the sound of this, especially as Michael was scowling.

"I have never...ever...slept with Hugo."

She mock slapped his arm as she sniggered.

"I'm very glad to hear it."

He leaned over her shoulder to look down the list.

"Ah. The Matrix; much more like it."

"You like the Matrix?"

"Doesn't everyone?"

"Well, I do. OK. That was easy."

And she flicked to the movie channel whilst Michael made a call.

Five minutes later there was a knock on their door, and a tray was produced with popcorn, fizzy drinks, sweets and ice cream. Michael tipped the guy and took the bounty to Amanda.

"Augh. I've only just had lunch," she groaned whilst clutching her full belly.

"You don't have to eat it all," he winked.

Another knock at the door interrupted them. Michael was up on his feet in a flash and cautiously approached the door. He shook his head as he opened it to Mark.

"Alright Twenty-nine?"

"Yes thanks. But you are supposed to be resting."

"I slept. Ooooh snacks," he exclaimed as he spied the goodies piled up on the bed.

"And The Matrix."

"Care to join us?" Amanda smirked.

"Oh, I'd hate to intrude," he said as he grabbed a handful of popcorn and settled into a chair.

Michael was actually relieved. Not jumping Amanda would be a whole lot easier with him here.

He pulled Amanda up to sit between his legs as his back rested against the headboard, so her head could rest on his chest. His arms wrapped around her, and he stroked her arm absentmindedly. She felt so right being this close to him. He kissed the top of her head.

"Less of that," came the voice from the nearby chair.

"Yes sir," Michael returned.

But Mark was actually really glad to see Michael like this. He knew Michael would still be through that connecting door before him if the alarm was raised, but for now he looked relaxed and happy. He didn't think he'd ever seen him like this. It was nice.

As the film flickered in the background they chatted about their day. Mark belly laughed at the 'Monster Child', but had to admit he probably would have done the same.

"I'm just glad it was only a kid. Mind you, there are few things in the world more deadly than children," he said with a wink.

"So what's the master plan for tonight? Please don't say a nightclub," Mark enquired.

"No. He seems quite happy with Claire. I'm hoping it will be quiet."

"So, what's your story, morning glory?" Amanda asked Mark.

"Oh no. No. I can't possibly tell you. It's classified."

"That good?"

"Just that bad."

"Am I allowed to know if you're actually British, as you sound? Or are you another covert spy?"

"Born and bred in Britain. Bit boring when you compare it to Mr World over there."

"There's nothing boring about that. So, how did you get into being the second Samurai?"

"Samurai?"

"Sorry. Apparently, she likes The Bodyguard, and thinks that's what our life is like," Michael apologised.

Mark groaned and threw popcorn at Amanda.

"Well, I won't learn if you don't tell me," she simpered.

"The truth is far less glamorous. It's a bit like watching paint dry."

"Wow. Thanks for the insight, Mark," Amanda said sarcastically.

"OK. Babysitting for adults then."

She threw popcorn back at him. The volley of popcorn was met with a veritable ambush as Mark scooped a handful back.

Michael leaped up and stood in front of Amanda, arms out wide, "Fear not, fair maiden. I shall protect you."

"No, brave knight. I cannot allow you to sacrifice yourself."

And she got up too, scooping more ammo and launching it at Mark, darting in front of Michael.

Mark seized the opportunity and went to scoop her up off her feet, but her foot caught him behind the legs, and he landed on his butt.

"What just happened?" Mark asked from the floor.

"The big shot, highly trained security operative just got bested by a girl," Michael laughed.

"Yeah, but what? When? What?"

"Yep. Bested by a girl," she chanted as she reached down to help him up.

"Where did you learn to do that?"

"Watching films."

"Really?"

"Nooo. I used to do Taekwondo," she confessed as she winked at him.

"Ever thought of making a career out of those moves?"

"Yeah, but the role of Jackie Chan was already taken."

"Ha ha. I'm serious."

"What, adult babysitting? How could a girl refuse when you make it sound so appealing?"

Michael's phone interrupted them. The two shot through next door.

"I heard a loud thud. Is everything OK?" Hugo asked, worried that there may have been an intruder after all.

"Sorry. Everything's fine. Mark just…err…fell over something."

"Well, OK. As you're here, can one of you take the girls back so they can collect some more stuff?"

"More?"

"Well, Claire wants to stay to dinner, so she needs clothes."

"Why don't they just bring all their stuff?" Mark's comment was meant to be sarcastic, but it earned him a 'good idea' from Hugo. Great, he'd had to open his big mouth.

Michael accompanied the girls back to their hotel so they could collect their things and check out. There were only a few nights left anyway, so they'd agreed they might as well stay in the hotel with the boys. It just saved all the toing and froing really.

Mark actually sat with them for dinner that night. And Michael had humbly asked at reception if they could send someone from housekeeping up, as their popcorn had been spilled. He didn't add it had been spilled by mischievous hands.

On their way back from dinner Mark paused in the reception area, and held Michael back with his hand on his arm.

"Dude. I got this. Go have some fun on your own." Michael started to try to protest, but Mark was insistent.

Well, he and Amanda hadn't really had any proper time on their own yet, had they? So Michael conceded.

The pair of them strolled down to the beach together arm in arm. It was dark, but the lights were shining out from the bars and restaurants that lined the beach.

Ordinarily, he would have worried more about their safety, but having seen her moves earlier, he was less concerned. Besides, he didn't have to protect anyone else right now, and he knew he could take care of himself.

Instead, he actually relaxed as they walked. They took their shoes off and walked barefoot across the sand, away from the night crowds.

"So, was it that bad?" Amanda asked him.

"Was what that bad?"

"Today?"

"Today was different."

"Different good?"

"Don't make me say it."

"I'm not making you say anything."

"Today was wonderful, because you were there. Happy now?"

"Blissfully."

"Good. I would have you so. I would always have you happy. I love your smile."

He bent down and quickly stroked her lips with his tongue.

"Be-have," she admonished playfully.

"Do I make you horny, baby?" he asked, mimicking her Austin Powers impression.

"Ho hooo, that's just wrong."

"What, that I make you horny?"

"No. That voice coming out of you."

"So, I do make you horny?"

His voice was now low and husky, as he stopped and looked her in the eyes. His hands tracing their now familiar path through her hair had her parting her lips in anticipation. But he didn't kiss her. He put his mouth close to hers but withdrew, driving her wild.

He went to walk off, but she caught his hand and pulled back. He let himself get drawn to her.

"Oh no you don't," she ordered, and commanded a kiss.

Her mouth was on his before he could run away again. But this time there was no fight. He just gave himself up to her. They lost themselves in the moonlight. He cleared his throat before he could speak.

"So, do you want to go to one of those bars?" he asked nodding in the general direction.

"Sure. We have all night, right?"

"Yes. Tonight I am a mouse, and the cat is on holiday."

His look was lecherous and hot as hell.

They found a bar that had a seat available where they had a view of the sea, and ordered vodka and Coke.

"I like that you like vodka," he commented.

"Oh, don't be so…"

"So?"

"So bloody stereotypically Russian."

"What? I like vodka. It is you who are assigning that to a nationality. I like to eat sausages and mash too; does that make me British?"

He was teasing her though. He knew exactly what she meant.

"So, Mr Alkaev, vot doo ve do tomorrow?" she said in Bond Russian.

"Tomorrow ve meet again. But I get to stroke *your* pussy," he replied in the same over-hammed accent.

"Oooh, I like that idea," she said, practically purring.

"But honestly? I don't know. I don't want to think about tomorrows. Right now we have tonight."

They sat there for a couple of hours, talking about everything and nothing, staring into the darkness over the water.

Neither of them could completely forget the pain that was soon to chase away this happy feeling. They were subdued as they started walking back to the hotel.

Suddenly he scooped her up and swung her round, making her cry out in surprise and delight.

"Enough, Pretty One. Enough sorrow. You should be happy."

And he whirled her round again, her legs flying out behind her, as he clung under her arms and around her back. She shrieked this time.

"Michael, put me down."

He did, but only so he could grab her waist and one of her hands, and dance her round in a circle. He released her, but she took a few steps forward in a ballet walk, culminating in her putting her hand against her forehead as ballerinas do in the 'I like him, but I'm running away, but should I' moments.

He cocked his head to one side before strutting up to her. What the hell? There was nobody else around in this part of town.

He went to take her hand, and to his astonishment, she jeté'd away from him. He leaped after her and caught her up in his arms, lifting her straight up in front of him. He put her down softly.

"What? You're the only one who learned ballet?" she preened.

"Did I forget to tell you my BA was in Dance & Drama?"

"You are just full of surprises."

"I like to keep you on your twinkle toes."

"Come. I am so going to sweep you off yours."

He hurried their pace as they walked the rest of the way back to the hotel.

He walked into his room, but halted, shielding Amanda with his body. Something was up. Someone was there, or had been. There was a glow shimmering through the otherwise dark room.

He peered around the corner and saw a myriad of candles illuminating the room, and rose petals on the bed.

There was a note stuck onto the mirror, 'Relax Romeo! Romance is courtesy of your local friendly Samurai. No intruder. Enjoy.'

He smiled at himself, and at the lovely gesture. Amanda was gazing open mouthed.

"Mark," he confirmed.

"That's just the loveliest thing," she sighed, moisture glistening in her eyes.

"I'd hate to waste this much effort."

"Well, naturally," she cooed, as she sashayed over to where her lover was standing.

The candlelight was infusing the atmosphere with its soft shimmer, and scenting it with warm spices.

As she stood there, she locked onto his eye contact, and with a naughty air, started slowly tugging her top off, and swirled it in the air in an enticing striptease.

Taking her lead, he unbuttoned his shirt, taking his time with each and every button.

She snaked her hips in a dance of seduction as she wriggled out of her skirt. She stepped out of it and away from him a little, and turned a small pirouette, culminating in an Arabesque pose for him in nothing but her underwear.

He pulled off his trousers, leaving him totally bare, as he sauntered over, pointing his toes, stretching his arms out in true Premier Danseur style, keeping his eyes on hers.

He palmed her waist, and reached up to unhook her bra with his free hand, kissing her as he did. He knelt down to pull her thong off with his teeth.

He lifted her carefully yet forcefully, allowing her to cocoon herself against him as he strode towards the bed where he laid her down gently.

His love making that night was gentle and intimate, given with long, slow, soothing, languishing strokes.

They both wanted to take their time, to cherish every sweet sensation, to prolong their contact.

As their bodies joined so did their souls. The whole world disappeared to them as they beheld only each other. Their kisses were deep and passionate. Amanda's back arched as she luxuriated in the comfort he was providing.

He stared down at her with those penetrating blue eyes of his, seeing her for all she was.

The candles were the only illumination and threw them into half shadows as they moved together in their dance of love.

His hand moved to her face as he took in all her beauty with wonder, needing to feel something tangible in his palm so he could believe it. She was easily the best thing that had ever happened to him, and he was enraptured. He deepened his kiss, sending tremors up his whole body, sending her reeling.

After nearly an hour of tenderness he sucked her neck quickly, breathing in her scent, letting it fill his nose before increasing his speed.

She felt the build-up of friction, the buzz humming through her core as their need intensified. Her hips rocked as she moved to his rhythm.

They climbed higher together, their bodies now straining for release. The rock and sway growing urgent now, she gripped onto him, urging him on.

Still looking into her eyes, he felt the strain increase until he could contain it no more. With a gasp he climaxed as she released her own cries of passion. Even his thrusts felt gentle and loving as he came.

He kissed her affectionately as they climbed back down, before pressing his forehead to hers and closing his eyes. He put his elbows on either side of her head and lowered his chest down a little.

His hands brushed her hair back, giving him better access to stroke her cheek, which was moist with tears.

"I love you," he whispered.

"I love you too," she breathed back.

Nobody had ever made her cry during sex before, but this experience had been so emotional, so loving and so much more meaningful than she'd ever felt she hadn't been able to stem the flow.

He rolled onto his back, and scooped her up on top of him, so she was draped over him like a blanket.

"Hey," he soothed, "hey. I'm here. It's OK."

"Sorry. I'm fine. It's just that was so...so...intense."

He kissed her before replying, "Yeah. It really was."

His own voice was shaky. He too was overcome by the same powerful emotions. He just wrapped his arms around her, holding her close. He planted a kiss on the top of her head and stroked her back in a long soothing motion.

He didn't know how long they'd been lying there when his phone buzzed. Amanda had fallen asleep, so he had to manoeuvre her off him carefully before pulling his boxers on.

He rushed through the door as if the hotel was on fire, and found Mark had got there just before him (he'd been in the room the other side to give Hugo and Claire alone time too).

"What? What?" the boys asked in harmony.

"Sorry. I just thought I heard a noise."

"Where? Where did it come from?" Michael quickly quizzed.

"The balcony."

The guys both ran up to the balcony doors. The lights were not on in the room so they could see out fairly easily.

They couldn't see anyone so they opened the door. As they did, a large seagull took flight from its perch on the balcony chair.

"Fuck," Mark huffed at Hugo.

"It was a fucking seagull."

Michael came in from the balcony after him, having double checked it was all clear.

"Sorry Michael. Sorry Mark," Hugo said rather pathetically.

Michael just shrugged it off.

"Quite a day, hey? First 'Monster Child' and now 'Intruder Seagull'."

"Guess this makes us even?" Hugo suggested.

"Yeah. Hey, I'd rather you called and it turned out to be nothing, than you not calling and it being something," Michael placated him.

"Thanks."

"No worries. Now I'm going back to bed. You OK Mark?"

"Yeah. Heart back in place."

"OK then. Night."

And with that Michael returned to Amanda. Bless. She'd managed to stretch out across the entire bed.

The candles had long since been blown out, but he found one and relit it. There was just enough light for him to see her. He sat there for ages just watching her sleep; she looked so peaceful and happy.

She reached out for him in her sleep and whimpered as her arm hit empty space. He quickly blew out the candle and slid into bed next to her.

He didn't have much room, but he didn't care. Her arm had stretched out over him, and he was in seventh heaven. He would move mountains to always be here at her side. He just had to figure out which mountains it was that needed to be moved.

How had he ever lived without her? She was funny, intelligent, beautiful, agile and liked vodka. He listened to her soft breathing as she slept, and gazed as his eyes grew accustomed to the dark.

He must've fallen asleep eventually as the light shining through the gap in the curtains woke him up. He was still on the very edge of the bed, but Amanda's arm was still draped across him. What he wouldn't give to wake up like this every morning.

Chapter 7

Amanda murmured as she started to wake up, and positively beamed as she realised Michael was under her arm and she looked into his admiring face.

"Good morning," he greeted her.

She let out a pleased yet sleepy 'mmmm'.

He smoothed her hair, soothing her as she came to. She snuggled up to him as he offered his arm for her to shmush under, so her head was on his chest, the covers pulled up to keep her warm against the air conditioning.

A tap on the interconnecting door disturbed their peace.

Michael was the one to shout out, "Come in."

Claire padded through in hotel issue slippers and dressing gown.

"Morning," she breezed as she perched on the end of the bed, earning her a smile from her friend.

"Hugo's really got into this 'living' thing apparently. Do you think it's too much to ask to go to the waterpark today?"

Her question was directed at Michael even though she was looking at Amanda.

"Actually, it could be quite fun," Michael assented, much to the girls' surprise.

Noting their expressions he added, "What? I'm not an ogre. The four of us can go together, masquerading as normal people."

This was said with a cheeky wink.

"There'll be lots of people there. Yeah. Why not?"

Claire was so happy she reached over for a group hug.

"Ooh," she uttered in appreciation of Michael's muscles before she realised what she was saying.

He just gave her one of his shy out of the corner of his mouth, lowered eyed grins with a sort of huffed laugh.

"Are you guys coming down to breakfast?" Claire asked.

"Ummm…I kind of have to. Part of the job description," Michael admitted.

"Oh right. Ummm…"

"His usual breakfast time is in half an hour, and I'll…we'll be there."

"Right you are then," Claire said as she shuffled back to Hugo's room.

"Come on then, sleepy one. We've been summoned."

He gently pushed Amanda to encourage her to get up.

She didn't want to budge, so he got up and went to her side of the bed and pulled back the bedclothes. She moaned at the cold and curled up.

He bent down and scooped her up in his arms and didn't put her down again until they were in the bathroom. He reached out to the shower controls, and turned it on but only at a tepid temperature.

"Aaaargh," she screeched as he pulled her in with him.

"It's not that cold. It'll help with your fatigue."

"It's *your* fatigue; you tired me out," she huffed, her bottom lip pouting.

He took that lip in his mouth and sucked it. That made her smile.

"There's my Pretty One. I love your smile."

"I'll smile more with coffee."

"And you'll have some soon. And then you can spend all day on a sun lounger if you don't want to follow Hugo onto waterslides."

He sounded concerned.

"I'm sorry. Am I being that grumpy? Honestly, just chuck some coffee into me and I'll be fine. Waterslides sound fun actually."

Within half an hour they were dried, dressed and delivering Hugo to breakfast. They all seemed hungry this morning; curious. Couldn't be the exercise they were all obviously getting, could it?

Amanda was smiling at the way her friend was grinning, apparently more than satisfied.

After breakfast, they stopped by their rooms to grab a few things, and so Michael could pop his head into Mark's room to check he was OK. He was staying behind again today, and Michael had brought up some bits from the restaurant for his friend who was enjoying his lie-in.

The two excited couples arrived at the waterpark, and were soon queuing to race down the multi-laned, multi-coloured slide.

The girls were squealing with laughter as they raced down. Amanda won (probably due to the fact she was also the lightest). Hugo demanded a rematch all the same.

They went up and down the slides for hours. They split into their couples to go down the black hole ride, where more screeching could be heard coming from the girls.

They worked their way up, finally daring each other to go down the 50ft free fall slide. The girls held hands as they waited, terrified but not wanting to back out and look like a complete chicken.

Of course, Michael had to go first. He waited down the bottom for the others. Hugo was next, thrilled at the exhilaration.

They heard Claire before they saw her, screaming at the top of her lungs as she careened down.

Amanda came down last, letting out a whoop as she 'landed'. Michael gave her a hug; proud at how they'd both taken on the challenge.

But after all the excitement they all agreed they were hungry so wandered to the restaurant to refuel. The afternoon was much quieter, as they lounged in a quiet area, soaking up the rays, occasionally striking up conversation.

Michael subtly held Amanda's hand in between their sunbeds, savouring the contact. Hugo was naturally the other side of him. He felt like he'd become closer to him at the same time as getting to know Amanda.

Hugo was a good bloke really. And being on holiday had really relaxed him; all signs of pretension and spoiled strops had now gone, leaving just the real him.

In amongst all the fun Michael hadn't forgotten this was their last day together. In all honesty, it was probably why he'd agreed to such a relaxed day of fun; he needed the distraction.

Amanda hadn't forgotten either. Especially as she laid there quietly in the sun.

Claire and Hugo were having fun, but that's all it was for them. They weren't serious about each other; it was purely a holiday romance. Hugo was enjoying his new found freedom, Claire was just having good sex.

Tomorrow was approaching all too soon. Amanda wasn't ready; they hadn't thought of a genius plan yet, how could she say goodbye to Michael without knowing when she'd see him again?

Panic lurched around in her stomach and stifled her breath which seemed to have got caught in her throat. Tomorrow she was going back home to her mundane life, to her mediocre flat, to eat miserable meals all on her fucking own. This wasn't fair. Stupid Russian.

Why couldn't he just happen to live down the road? Or London? At least the same pissing country. But no, soon there'd be about 2,000 miles between her and the man of her dreams. Oh sweet mercy; two *thousand* miles. She let out a muffled sob as tears ran down her tanned cheeks.

Michael was suddenly sitting on the side of her lounger, looking tenderly down at her, concern written across his face.

"Oh God. Amanda. I'm so sorry. I wanted you to be happy, but now I think maybe it would have been better for you never to have met me."

"No. No. Never say that," she all but yelled at him in alarm.

"Not even next week?"

"Not even then. Especially not then. It's just I don't know what to do. My flat is going to be so empty, my bed will be cold. And I have no hope of ever seeing you again."

Instead of being able to offer any words of comfort whatsoever all Michael could do was let his own tears fall. She clung onto him, trying to bury her head in his shoulder.

"There'll be two thousand miles and goodness knows how many countries between us. And I don't know what to do," she sobbed.

The hurt in her eyes was obvious, the air around them was black with their sorrow.

Hugo got up with Claire so they could make a discreet exit to give them some privacy.

"Stay the fuck where you are," Michael commanded, not even having to look behind him.

"Michael. Sorry. I thought you'd want some space."

"Yes, but I'm still on duty, so I'm stuck with you. So sit the fuck down."

His tone was one of silent menace as he barked his orders over his shoulder. Amanda was suddenly seeing how lethal he could be, but she'd already seen that the night of the almost mugging.

She wasn't afraid of him. Neither was Hugo, although he did sit back down quite quickly, and turned his back to them to face Claire who'd also descended rather rapidly.

"Amanda. We will find a way."

He had turned back to her, and was looking at her earnestly.

"I don't know yet, but we'll think of something."

"I'm sorry. I know I'm not supposed to be hearing this, but my father does a lot of business in London. Maybe I can ask to accompany him, so that I can learn more about the business first hand? Meet his clients? Michael would have to come too. I could stay for a while each time?" Hugo offered hopefully.

"There. You see? We can come over on a business trip."

"But I don't live in London."

"No, but we can come to see you."

"Is this it? Is this our future? Ships passing in the night from time to time?"

"Amanda, please. We're just trying to think of solutions here. It's a start isn't it?"

"Yeah, I guess. I'm sorry, Michael. Sorry Hugo. I don't mean to be so needy, but I just can't face going back."

"Then don't."

"What?"

"Don't get on that plane, Amanda. Get on ours."

"You're mad."

"Possibly, but come home with me."

"And do what? I don't speak Russian, so I'm fairly sure that rules me out of working there, or pretty much living there."

"Oh fuck, it's hopeless. Amanda, I love you."

"I love you, Michael."

"Then we'll find a way to be together."

Hugo and Claire were devastated for their friends. It really did seem hopeless for them. Life was just too cruel.

They hit the showers, the girls hugging each other.

"Amanda. I'm so sorry. I don't know what to say."

"No. I'm sorry. I didn't mean to fall apart like that."

"What else could you do? Amanda, I'm just amazed you've held it together this long. Just know I'm here, OK? Do you want me to come home with you when we get back? I don't think you should be on your own."

"Would you? I'd really appreciate that. I've got a feeling this is going to be a bumpy landing."

The boys weren't doing much better. Hugo was locking forearms with Michael in his show of solidarity.

"If you need time off to go see her, you know that's OK?"

"Thanks. I might take you up on that."

Having got changed, the four met by the exit.

"Right, time for some drinks, I think," Hugo announced.

They wandered towards the beach and found a bar. The nearest one; they weren't feeling fussy. Naturally, Champagne was ordered.

Mark was on his way. Michael had phoned him with their location, knowing he wanted to get absolutely slaughtered tonight.

"*Za vas*," the boys toasted their girls.

"Zah VAHS," the girls tried in return, earning them a small cheer.

After his first glass of Champagne Michael beckoned a waiter over.

He handed over a fist of notes with a desperate look as he asked, "*Si us plau, puc tenir una ampolla de vodka?*"

A few minutes later a whole bottle of vodka and some shot glasses were placed on the table.

The boys attacked theirs straight away, "za lyoo-bóf" they hailed (to love) as they downed their shots.

Hugo's toast was more wishing his protector luck in love after what he'd witnessed this afternoon.

The girls soon joined them in their vodka shots, but after wincing the first one down Claire returned to the Champagne.

Amanda however tried to keep up with the boys. She held her own for quite some time, but they proved to be too much for her in the end. Michael ordered some snacks to help soak up some of the alcohol. Just as well, as she went into rambling mode as they were waiting for the food to arrive.

"I love you, Mikhail Alky…Alk…eye…ev," she was really slurring and louder than she intended.

"OK. I love you too, but the whole bar doesn't have to know."

"When I get home I'm going to dream of you eeeevery night, and think of you aaaall daaay."

"You will never leave my thoughts either."

"I'm going to make a little Michael shrine."

"OK, that's just a bit creepy."

"I'll pray to it every night before I go to sleep."

"I tell you what you're going to do."

"Don't you tell me what to do, Mr Bossy Pants."

"You'll go home and you'll email me each day. And we can talk on the phone sometimes. And every time I hear your voice it will be as if you're by my side where you belong. And I'll be able to sleep, knowing you're somewhere in the world thinking of me as much as I'm thinking of you."

"Awwww. You say the sweetest things. Have I told you how much I love you?"

"Oh look, food's here," he said gratefully, feeding her some snacks.

When the food ran out they all went for a walk along the beach to clear their heads a bit, before heading back to the hotel. Mark made sure they were in their rooms safely.

"Amanda, I may not have a chance to say tomorrow, so I'd like to wish you a safe journey. It's been great meeting you. And I know it doesn't feel possible now, but I'm sure we'll meet again soon," Mark said as he gave her a hug before heading to his own room.

Both Amanda and Michael felt a bit fuzzy after their heavy drinking session, but the walk had helped.

Her stomach went into free-fall again as she thought about their parting. She pulled Michael close to her and kissed him with all the longing she felt.

"I'm coming with you to the airport tomorrow. Mark's staying here with Hugo. OK?"

"No. Not OK. But only because I don't want to leave you. Thanks for coming with me."

"It's OK. We're going in style in the hotel's car. And Mark's right. We will be together again soon. Somehow. Even if I have to quit my job."

"Quit? But you love your job. I can't make you do that."

"Let's just say I'm considering it. I've done my travelling, and had some amazing clients. I've no idea what else to do, but I'm at least thinking about it."

All she could do was hug him as tears sprang to her eyes again.

"Shhh…" he soothed.

He kissed her cheek and rubbed the back of her head. She moved so she could kiss his luscious lips, gently at first, but then with a growing need, catching her breath.

"I'm going to miss you so much."

"I'm going to miss you too. I love you."

He regained the kiss, deepening it. His hands were at her back, drawing her against him. They both needed this parting gift to each other.

They stripped quickly, their hands crawling over their bodies, trying to hold on to the hope they were so desperate to find, trying to latch on to these precious moments.

Amanda laid on the bed with Michael sidling up to her. As he kissed her his fingers worked their way down her body, before finding her slit. His fingers trailed slowly up and down, feeling her silky moistness. Feeling how much she wanted him, how much he meant to her.

His mouth left hers as he kissed every inch of her; implanting memories. He wanted to remember what she felt like, what she smelled like, what she tasted like. His other hand raked through her hair as he nuzzled it.

His tongue licked around her ears and down her neck, where he sucked. He kissed her shoulders and arms, sucking each of her fingers languorously. He smooched her breasts, licked down her torso, across her hips, down her thighs all the way down to sucking her toes.

He kissed his way back up to the apex of her thighs where he flicked his tongue around her nub, sending pulses through her core. He lapped at her, revelling in the taste of her.

Amanda felt tingles all over. Her need increased as he lingered. His index finger plunged into her as his tongue continued its assault. Her orgasm flooded her system, sending her reeling.

He moved himself to lay on top of her. As he slid his cock inside her, Amanda stretched her legs out and up, so they were resting in a 'V' on his shoulders, giving him greater access. She wanted to feel him as much as she could, to remember this moment forever. Needing to imprint it in her memories, so she could cling to it in her loneliness.

He thrust forwards, making her tremor with the thrill.

She was so full of him it bordered on pain. She gripped onto his lower back as he continued his powerful pushes. She looked up into his eyes, falling into their oceanic blue, drowning in him.

He was looking through her hazel eyes into her soul. They were united mind, body and soul. Their limbs locked together in this torturous ride of love, lust and life. She wanted to stay in this moment forever, to just freeze time now.

She grabbed onto his lower back, urging him on. His thrusts got faster and more heated, the urgency increasing inside both of them. Their muscles clenching in that oh so sweet momentum.

Michael's head was thrown back as he came hard and fast. Amanda's hips rose to get her fill of him. Oh bliss. Sweet heavenly release.

She cried out her orgasm as he groaned through his. As his pulses slowed and she lowered her legs, he looked down at her through his sweaty blonde mane.

He rolled onto his side, and their limbs intertwined so they could hold each other as close as they could. How were they going to bear the sorrow of tomorrow? There were no words now, nothing to say. Nothing could describe their feelings any better than the act of love they'd just performed. They just lay like that until sleep overtook them.

The alarm woke them early the next morning. The girls' bags were packed. Claire kissed Hugo goodbye in his room. She too felt a pang at leaving, but it was nothing compared to the devastation exploding in Amanda's heart.

They trudged down the corridor for the last time. They collected a packed breakfast at reception, and wandered out to the awaiting car. The drive seemed to last an eternity, and Michael didn't let go of Amanda all the way; she was tucked under his arm.

But they arrived at the airport at last. The two lovers felt their hearts being ripped out of them, all the joy being sucked out of their entire being as they got out of the car.

"I can't come in with you. If I go any further I'm not going to want to leave that airport," Michael announced into her hair as they clung together as long as they could.

He 'wiped some dust out of his eye'.

"I feel like I should be saying some Bogart shit right now."

"No. No hill of beans. But I do have to get on that plane. I wish I didn't. I will always love you, Michael."

"This is NOT goodbye! You hear me?"

"Then why does it feel that way?"

"Because it just seems that way now. But it's not. I PROMISE you we'll meet again soon. You have my word."

Their foreheads were touching as they exchanged their vows of tomorrows to come, and their tears flowed like rivers. They kissed desperately, as though their lives depended on it.

"Amanda." Claire interrupted. "Honey, we have to go now."

"I know," she nodded sadly.

She touched that bristled cheek one more time, gave him one last kiss before she tore herself away.

She walked through the doors to the airport supported by her friend.

He watched as she went through the portal, heading back to her own life before he turned away to start walking towards the car.

He paused and turned as she came running back out and fell into his arms.

"I can't go," she cried.

"Amanda. Oh my Amanda."

He held her close as he tried in vain to regain his composure.

"My Pretty One, you have to go. But I will come to you soon. Go. Go on. I'll speak to you soon. Phone me as soon as you're through customs back home."

He almost shoved her away, and then she disappeared back into the airport.

She found Claire in the check-in queue. She wrapped a consoling arm around Amanda.

"Oh honey, you'll see him again. You will."

Michael's face was covered in the trails of his tears as the car drove him back to the hotel.

The girls wandered through the airport in a daze, and just sat down in the departure lounge waiting for their flight.

They barely noticed boarding. Claire even forgot to be scared as they prepared for take-off. Amanda downed a miniature vodka as soon as the drinks trolley came round when they were airborne. It took a tiny bot of the edge off, but she still felt like she was in hell.

The flight which had seemed so quick on the way out now felt like it spanned a lifetime as it took her away from the man she had to be with. But it did finally end, and they trundled through customs and baggage reclaim.

Amanda's phone was in her hands as soon as she was cleared to make calls and she could get a signal.

"I'm in the airport," she mumbled.

"Good. I'm glad you're there safely. I miss you already."

"How's Hugo?"

"He's in his room. I'm in mine. He's letting me have my space, I think."

"That's nice," she said absently.

"Will you call me when you get home? Or text? I'll call you back."

"OK. Bye for now."

"*Do svidaniya*."

Amanda leaned on their luggage trolley as she and Claire made their way to the shuttle bus to the car park.

Claire was luckily on Amanda's insurance, so she drove them home in deafening silence. She switched car radio on to fill the cavernous void.

When they got home they dumped their cases down and reached for the alcohol. Amanda sneered as she pulled out the bottle of vodka. She downed a shot before sending her text to Michael. Ten seconds later he was phoning her.

"You're home?"

"Yes."

"Good. OK. We can do this."

But he was trying to convince himself more than her.

"This is going to be fine. Right now I feel as if I have all my limbs missing but we'll be OK. It's just an adjustment."

He didn't sound right; slightly slurred.

"Have you been drinking?"

"My buddy Smirnoff is keeping me company, yes."

"Huurgh," she half laughed, "I have his cousin right here."

She started laughing, "God. We're not going to turn into alcoholics, are we?"

"I hope not," he began laughing too.

Not that there was anything funny in that. His laughter was like an angel singing in her ears, and Amanda began to laugh more. It lapsed into hysteria, and they both knew it.

"Why are we laughing?" she breathed through bursts of giggles.

"Because it beats crying."

And with that sobering thought they stopped and took deep breaths.

"Love you."

"Love you too. I think we better say goodbye there before this laps into madness again."

"I think you're right."

"But I am looking forward to talking to you tomorrow night. I might be up for phone sex by then."

"Oooh. That's a new one on me, I've not done that before. I'll look forward to it."

"Bye for now Pretty One."

"By my love."

Claire was on hand with a refill as soon as the call ended. Amanda necked it. She did not want to cry again.

She eventually staggered into bed that night, hoping she'd had enough vodka to knock her out. But she'd failed.

As she lay there in the cold empty darkness of her room those unwanted tears beckoned anyway.

All week she'd been nestled up to a gorgeous warm body, and now there was a chasm. Her phone buzzed, alerting her of a text message.

"My bed's empty without you and I can't sleep."

Michael was feeling this as much as she was.

"Mine too. I miss you so much it hurts. And I can't stop crying," she sent back.

"Hugo's going home next week. I'll make sure he's OK, and then I'll come to see you. Maybe in three weeks?"

"That sounds good. You sure it's OK?"

"He's already said yes."

"OK. I think I can sleep knowing that. Thank you. Love you. Night. xx"

"Night xx"

Sleep didn't come immediately, but it didn't take too long now Amanda had some hope.

Claire tidied up the sofa bed in the lounge in the morning and shoved some toast at Amanda, telling her she had to eat *something*.

She managed to swallow the buttered toast and some coffee before heading into work with Claire at her side. She was so glad her friend was there. She wasn't sure she would have managed to get out of bed at all today without her.

Claire fielded off the 'how was your holiday' questions from their colleagues. She merely said they'd had a lovely time, and the weather had been lovely. She covered Amanda's grim look by saying she'd picked up a tummy bug, and was still feeling a bit rough.

The mountain of emails was almost welcome today, as Amanda sifted through them on autopilot. It distracted her thoughts of Michael enough, but wasn't overly taxing, so she didn't have to apply too much effort to the work at hand.

Over in Ibiza, Hugo was having another quiet day, and all three lads were lounging by the pool. Michael was resisting the temptation to email Amanda. He didn't think it had been possible to feel this much loss.

It was like someone had switched off the light in his life. He yearned for Amanda; for her eyes, for her smile, for her funny comments, for her conversation, and yes, for her body.

Walking away from that airport was the hardest thing he'd ever had to do. He was seriously considering not being a 'bodyguard' anymore. But what the hell else could he do? It was the only job he'd really ever done.

It's not like he could wander into an office instead. And manned guarding at an office block was really a different beast, and he didn't see himself doing that either. He wanted something active. His thoughts were interrupted by Mark.

"Hey. How you doing?"

"I'm fine."

"You wanna tell your face? You've had the same brooding look all day."

"I'm just thinking."

"Ahh. That would be it. I thought it looked painful. Is that steam coming out of your ears?" Mark chuckled.

"Gee, thanks."

But the sarcastic comment had curled the corners of his mouth a little. He sighed as he laid his head back down on the lounger. It was nearly lunchtime, and he just couldn't resist it any more. He fired off an email from his phone.

"My darling Pretty One. I hope your day is going well. I am sitting in the sun, pining for my love."

The email hit Amanda's inbox, making her heart skip a beat.

She quickly replied, "It could be worse. Work is distracting me a little, but I am still missing you with every breath. And it's raining outside."

"It's nice to hear you, even in an email. You don't feel so far away like this. It won't be too long before I can come and see you."

"It better not be. I better get back to work, before my boss catches me. I'll speak to you tonight. Thanks for being there. Xx"

Claire dragged her out to lunch not long after that.

"How you holding up, Honey?" she asked as they walked up the road.

"Could be worse. He emailed just now."

"Is that better or worse?"

"Both. It was nice to hear from him, but it just reminded me how far away he is. But he reckons he's going to see me in a few weeks, once Hugo's safely installed back in his home properly."

"Well, that's good, isn't it?"

"Yeah. But does it sound spoiled if I say it's not enough?"

"No. I know what you mean."

And she reached an arm round her friend as she guided her into the café to eat something unhealthy.

The rest of the day passed in quiet contemplation but without incident. That night Amanda's phone rang and she virtually leapt on the thing.

"Hi," she said, sounding like an excited puppy.

"Hiii," he drooled. "Is Claire still there?"

"Yeah."

"Go into your room on your own then, Pretty One."

There was a predatory growl to his voice. She obeyed, shutting the door behind her. Claire politely turned the volume up on the TV and zoned out.

"Have you some music in your room?" he inquired.

"Yeah."

"Put it on."

'Buttons' by the Pussycat Dolls started up on her iPod speakers.

"Nice choice," he approved. "Go sit on the bed."

She wasn't used to taking orders, but these were more than OK. Frankly, it was hot as fuck. Her hands were already trembling.

"Put me on loud speaker on your phone, but not too loud," he continued.

"Done," she confirmed after a little fumbling with the screen and buttons.

"What are you wearing?"

"My work blouse and skirt."

"Oooh that will never do. Isn't that blouse a little warm for the heat in your flat?"

"Now you come to mention it, it is a little stuffy. I should take it off."

"That's my girl. Start with the top button; I want your breasts to show first."

She undid each button, providing a running commentary as she did. She heard his sharp intake of breath as she let her blouse fall. The visual memory of her was so strong it was like she was standing in front of him.

"That skirt's a little tight too, isn't it?"

"Mmmm…" she purred and unzipped it for him, and wriggled out of it.

"Aaarrrhhh…" he moaned, as he 'saw her' standing in nothing but her underwear.

He was touching himself, and told her so. That sent a spike of frisson through her.

"Take off your bra for me, Amanda."

As she did she earned an, "Oh yeeeaaah," from him.

"Now touch your breasts, hold them in your palms. How do they feel?"

She described the sensations, getting another groan of pleasure from the phone.

"Imagine I'm sucking them, naughty girl."

It was her turn to moan now.

"Let your hand go down your beautiful body like it wants to. Yeah, like that. Is that your panty line?"

"I can feel the lacy edge under my fingertips."

"Let your hand slip under and explore, beautiful."

They both moaned their pleasure at this.

"I'm already so wet for you," she murmured.

"My fingers are sliding up and down me. Aaahh. I'm slick with my desire for you."

"Take off your underwear, baby girl."

She obeyed.

"Mmmm...what a view," he whispered, closing his eyes imagining her legs beckoning him.

"Feel my tongue on you where your fingers are, Pretty One. Rub harder."

Her moans were increasing now.

"That's it, Baby. Feel me there."

His hand was stroking his cock faster.

"Yeah. That's it. Put a finger inside you now. Amanda; I'm inside you. I can feel my cock sliding in and out of your pussy. Oh, Amanda. You feel so good. Can you feel me?"

"Yes, Michael. Yes. Auuugghhh!"

"Feel me pushing into you; faster."

They were close now.

"Faster."

He heard her groaning, on the edge now.

"Come for me, Amanda."

It was the final command she needed. She orgasmed with the memory of him inside her. The sound of her crying out his name sent him over the edge into his climax too. They lay there panting, Christina Aguilera was singing 'Dirrty' on her iPod.

"My beautiful, dirty Amanda," she heard him whisper.

"That was amazing."

"Pretty good this end too. Thank you."

"Thank you. But I wish you were really here."

"Me too. I will be soon though."

"I know. It's the only thing getting me through this."

"I hate to shag and run, but I need to get ready. Hugo's not had dinner yet."

"OK. Say hi to Jorge for me."

"I will. I think even he's missing you."

"Really?"

"You touch so many lives without knowing it, Pretty One."

She giggled shyly.

"Love you. Night night."

"Night, my love."

The next day at work was a little easier thanks to the sexy episode last night. Amanda wriggled in her work chair each time she thought of it, and smiled wryly.

Tears still sprang to her eyes as Susan Boyle sang 'I Dreamed a Dream' on the car stereo on the way home. Yep; that summed it up. This hell she was now living. Caught in limbo between the love she had felt to the nothingness here and now.

Chapter 8

The rest of the week ran on in the same haze. Amanda got up, went to work, cheered up briefly at the odd email from Michael, fell back into a low slump until she had his evening phone call, then she slept. Repeat.

Claire was still with her, chucking food into her, to ensure she still ate. She was also pretty good at the hugs and the shoulder to cry on routine too.

Amanda had cried until she didn't think she could cry any more, and beyond. She felt ridiculous, but the harder she tried not to, the more she wept. It got a little easier, but still she missed him like the deserts miss the rain.

And now Michael was boarding his own plane, going even further away from her. Michael almost saw his heart where he'd left it at the airport as they approached the doors. Mark's hand was on his shoulder briefly.

Hugo's dad was using his jet, so they were using a commercial airline. Michael wasn't overly happy, but he was making it as secure as possible.

He had the VIP exit lined up at the other end, having spoken to an ex colleague of his in Domodedovo airport in Moscow.

He was on alert in the airport in Ibiza, but was able to relax enough once on the plane to mope a bit more.

He'd been perfectly happy and content with his life before Amanda had come leaping in. Now? Now it felt like the last thing he wanted.

He resented anything that kept him from her. He'd been tetchy all week, and the guys had tried to leave him be as much as they could.

Hugo had certainly not ventured any bright ideas for sightseeing, so had spent a really boring week in the hotel.

Hugo was missing Claire a bit. His freedom didn't seem to mean the same without her brightening up his life. He wasn't pining for her, but he had no inclination to go out and find a replacement just yet either. And now he was heading back home. Not much fun to be had there.

He wasn't going to be able to go back to the iron bar routine though. He was going to have to speak to his father about relaxing the rules a bit.

He understood the need for protection, but it was time he started to live too. This holiday had taught him that.

Mark was just hoping that whatever Michael did he'd be able to follow. They'd become good friends over the years, and didn't want to start over with a new work partner now. He knew how Michael worked, knew what was expected of him. It was a good position to be in.

They all had uncertain thoughts of a new future as the plane touched down in Moscow. The VIP Meet & Greet lady welcomed them at the plane.

"Good afternoon gentlemen. I hope you had a good flight. This way please," she said in Russian, leading the way past the crowds filing off.

They were given the fast-track route through border control, and were made to feel welcome in the VIP lounge as a porter collected their baggage for them.

Michael hated airports, and this was no exception. He just wanted to get Hugo home so he could talk to Amanda. He sent her a text to let her know they'd landed.

At last the porter emerged with their bags, and they followed the 'Meeter & Greeter' to the exit, where Hugo's chauffeur driven car was waiting a short distance off, down the bottom of the steps.

Lazy arsehole hadn't gotten out the driver's door yet though. He knew better than that.

He could see them from where he was, surely? Michael had even text him to say they were on their way. He should be in sight.

The hairs on the back of Michael's neck were sticking up, as he sensed the first signs of protocol not being observed.

He shot a glance across to Mark, who was tensing too. So, not just his own paranoia then.

A man suddenly rushed at them from behind the column to their right.

"Down down down!" shouted Mark.

They went into a crouch, but it was too late. The man had grabbed Hugo's arm as he tried to duck, and was dragging him off. Fuck. Just fuck.

How was this happening? How did that guy know he was there? And who the fuck was he?

He saw the 'Meet & Greet' take her place next to the assailant. Fucking bitch. Shit! They'd walked straight into this one.

The guy had a gun pointed at Hugo's back. Michael could do fuck all from where he was.

He prayed to God that the cameras above his head hadn't been disabled as he got onto his knees, holding his hands above his head.

"*Stop!*" he yelled loudly in Russian.

That got the guy's attention.

"Stop," he repeated.

"I cannot allow you to do this."

"Do what?" the kidnapper sneered.

Michael tried his best to sound humble. The scared bit wasn't so challenging.

"Please. Please don't hurt him. I can't let you take my bodyguard."

"Bodyguard? Fuck off!"

Hugo himself managed to turn in the guy's arms.

"What the fuck are you doing?" he shouted in English.

That seemed to lend some credence to Michael's statement though.

"I'm presuming you're after me, not him. I don't think his life is worth much. I'm Dimitri Krylov."

"Bullshit. He was in the middle."

"Of course he was. If I was in the middle it would have been a bit obvious, wouldn't it?"

The kidnapper was coming round to the idea. Shit. He would be killed himself if he returned with the wrong target.

"Did you hear their names?" he asked the not so friendly greeter.

"He called him Hugo," she observed, pointing at Hugo (the real Dimitri).

"Fuck. You could have said before."

"I thought he was bluffing," she defended.

He shoved Hugo away from him but raised his gun at Michael's chest. Hugo tried not to run as he reached Mark's side.

They had the high ground now, but no weapons to retaliate with.

"You. Down here. Now. Slowly," the kidnapper commanded.

"OK. OK. Please just don't shoot," Michael snivelled.

The twat was actually buying this shit. If he could get close he had a chance of disarming they guy, who was now confused and off balance because of that.

The bitch on the other hand was reaching round her back. Fuck. She was packing too. Michael slowly started to stand, hoping to buy some time.

He sank back down to his knees as yeah, she pulled out a 9mm handgun too. Oh shit, this could get messy.

"Please don't shoot me. Don't shoot," he cried in a performance worthy of an Oscar.

"Just do what I say. Nobody needs to get hurt here."

He looked at the two 'bodyguards'.

"You two; on the floor, hands on your head."

Mark not seeing any better options took the lead and started sinking down, nudging Hugo to follow.

The guy's gun was still pointed at Michael's chest.

"You. Get back up on your fucking feet."

"Halt! Police!"

The cry came from the bottom of the steps off from the side. The cavalry had arrived.

Armed airport police started swarming in. Thank the lord for CCTV and alert officers looking at the monitors.

But Michael fell back onto the marble as a shot rang out.

The attacker had panicked at the police cry and pulled his trigger. Closely followed by a shot from the police, shooting the guy's arm.

The bitch had dropped her weapon in horror. Shit. This was all going wrong. She felt the policeman almost break her arms behind her back as she face planted the floor. Her accomplice was getting similar treatment.

Mark was by Michael's side in an instant.

"Guard down! I need an ambulance," he cried out to the Russian police.

He ripped off his jacket and held it against Michael's chest to stop the bleeding. Fuck, there was blood flowing out of him badly.

"Michael. Michael. Stay with me buddy. You're going to be OK."

"What the fuck?"

"Shh. Don't talk. You've been shot. An ambulance is on its way. Hugo's safe. The police are doing their job. It's going to be OK."

"Oh god, Amanda. Tell her I love her always."

He felt his energy starting to ebb away.

"You can tell her yourself. No fucking goodbyes here mate. No fucking way. Stay with me."

The paramedics arrived. Thankfully they had a base at the airport, so arrived very quickly indeed. The police nodded them through and they strode up the steps.

"What do we have?"

"9mm handgun, bullet wound through the chest. Bullet's hit the door behind him, so I'm hoping it's a clean hit. Blood loss is severe. His name's Michael. Thirty years old. Russian."

Hugo translated all that quickly into Russian, as Mark's wasn't up to the task. The paramedic glanced at the shattered glass behind them.

One of the paramedics was kneeling by him and holding his hand.

"OK. Mikhail. Can you hear me?"

His eyes flickered a little, and he managed a groan.

"We're just going to put a pressure bandage on your chest here. OK?"

They worked quickly. The team rolled him onto a back board as quickly and gently as they could, and put a c-collar on him and hooked him up with high flow oxygen, a chest drain and IVs.

The paramedic was talking to him the whole time.

"Are you on any medication, Michael?"

"No," he groaned.

"On a scale of one to ten, ten being worst pain in your life, what is your pain level?"

"Ten."

"Do you have any allergies?"

"Only to bullets," he quipped huskily.

"When was the last time you ate or drank anything?"

"Breakfast, this morning. Aaaarrrrgh."

"You're doing really well, Mikhail. Sorry; we're just lifting you onto the trolley. We'll be on our way soon."

A blanket was pulled over his now naked chest. Mark and Hugo were by his side as he was loaded into the ambulance. Mark saw the police arresting the would-be kidnappers and the driver of the car as they walked over.

"That's not our chauffeur! Hugo; tell them to check the boot. Fuck."

Hugo translated quickly as they clambered in with their friend. Mark was holding Michael's hand as he sat down next to him.

"You're gonna be OK now, buddy. If you close those baby blues I'm going to kiss you, so you just stay awake for me. Hear me?"

Michael managed a grimace of a smile.

"Stay the fuck away from my mouth, princess."

"Stay the fuck awake then," Mark said with a wink.

Chapter 9

There was a hospital mercifully close, and Michael was rushed in with paramedics giving stats and details at the awaiting crew. A kind looking nurse showed Mark and Hugo to a quiet waiting room.

"Can I use a phone in here?" Hugo asked.

"Yes. In here you can. There's a vending machine up the hall if you want drinks," she replied as she discreetly left them alone.

Hugo had picked up Michael's abandoned jacket which thankfully had his mobile phone in it. He found Amanda's name and hit dial.

"Hello gorgeous. I'm so glad you rang. I just had the weirdest feeling," she sighed.

"Amanda. It's Dimitri."

"Who?"

Shit, his brain was really fried with shock.

"Hugo. It's Hugo. Amanda. *Yob!* Michael's been hit. We're at the hospital. *Govno!* I don't know what to say."

"What? What do you mean hit?"

Mark had grabbed the phone.

"Amanda. It's Mark. We were attacked at the airport. Your man played hero and took a bullet. He's getting treatment now. He was calling out for you as they wheeled him off. I think you should get here."

"Fuck. Mark. Is he OK? Shit. I don't know what to do."

She was panicking.

Hugo was back on the phone.

"Amanda. Where do you live?"

She told him.

"My father has the jet in London. I'll get him to send it over. Can you get to _ airfield?"

"I'll be there. Somehow. I'll get there."

"His pilot's name is Henry. Do not get in with anyone else. Hear me?"

"Hugo. I'm scared."

"It's OK. The attackers have been arrested. Mark's here with me. I'll get someone to meet you at the airfield here, and I'll text you his name once I've arranged it. Michael will probably kill me for bringing you here, but I agree with Mark. Amanda; you need to be prepared. It looked serious."

Her breath caught in her throat.

"Can Claire come?"

"Under the circumstances it's not a good idea. We'll look after you. I promise. Just get here."

"OK. I'm leaving for the airfield now."

She hung up the phone. She was still at work.

"Fuck. Amanda; what's wrong?" Claire asked as soon as she saw her friend's ghostly white face.

"Michael's..." her voice came out in a wail, "Michael's been shot."

"Amanda. No. Shit. No. Is he OK?"

"I don't know," she sobbed.

"Hugo's sending a jet. I've got to get to _ airfield. He said to prepare for the worst."

She could barely breathe for crying as the sobs now shook her body. Claire had rushed round the desk and grabbed her in her arms.

"Oh my God. OK. Let's get you airborne."

She grabbed their bags and coats and frogmarched Amanda over to their boss' desk.

"Amanda's got a family emergency, Frank. I'm taking her to the hospital."

"Of course. Is there anything I can do?"

"No. But she might need some time off."

"Yes yes. Fine."

He could see the obvious panic.

"I'll fill you in on the details tomorrow."

"Please. Just do what you need to do. I'm sorry, Amanda. I hope whatever it is turns out OK. Take as much time as you need. Don't worry about here."

And with that they made a dash for the exit. They stopped off at the flat. Amanda hadn't unpacked properly yet, so Claire managed to chuck some clothes in her case, not quite sure what she'd need, so she included some sweaters just in case.

She drove hell for leather to the destination marked on the Sat Nav. She dumped the car, and led Amanda up to the building and asked if _ plane was there.

They were pointed in the right direction, having had an ID check. Claire grabbed a vended tea en route and shoved it into Amanda's hand.

"Hello, Miss Amanda. I am Henry."

The pilot with a strong Russian accent greeted her. Claire gave her a quick hug as Amanda clambered on board.

"He'll be fine, sweetie. Just go to him. He'll want to see you when he wakes up. I'll be praying for you guys."

"Thanks."

And with that the door was closed, and she was shown a seat and strapped in.

"We'll be in Moscow in approximately four hours. If you need anything I'll be through there," Henry said as he pointed towards the cockpit.

"Thank you."

They were soon taking off. It was a lot bumpier than she was used to, but she barely noticed.

She fretted the whole journey. She offered up prayers to every deity she could think of.

"Just please let him be OK. Please let him be OK."

What would she do if he died? No; she couldn't bear to think of that. He just had to be OK. Yes, he was going to be OK. She may not be; she was driving herself crazy.

She thought she'd been in hell just being without him? What the fuck had she known? *This* was hell. Oh shit, please let him be OK. Deep breaths; just take deep breaths, she reminded herself.

After an eternity the plane landed in Moscow. She was met by Radimir, the driver Hugo had texted her about. Her prayers and worry continued in the car.

When she got to the hospital she flew inside, her suitcase trailing behind her. She approached the desk. Shit, she couldn't speak Russian. How on earth did she say 'I'm looking for my boyfriend who's been shot?'

"Ummm…Hello. Ummm…Michael Alkaev?"

"Hello. You must be Amanda. His friends said you'd be arriving."

Oh thank fuck for that! She could kiss the English speaking nurse.

"Is Michael OK?"

"I'm afraid I don't know. His friends are still in the waiting room through there," she said as she pointed the way.

Amanda ran in the direction of the nurse's finger. The boys looked up as she burst into the room. They looked dreadful. Hugo's arms were around her before she knew what was happening.

"Hugo. Oh Hugo. Is he OK?"

"We're still waiting for news. Amanda I'm so glad you're here."

"Hi Amanda," Mark said meekly.

"I'm so sorry. He was so brave, but it should have been me. How I wish I'd taken that bullet."

She went over and hugged him.

"I know you did everything you could, Mark."

He squeezed her back.

"Can I get you anything? There's a hideous vending machine that dispenses tar tea if you want?"

"Yeah. Tea would be good thanks."

She collapsed into a chair, with Hugo joining her to squeeze her hand and giving it a gentle kiss. He didn't let go until Mark handed her the steaming cup of fluid that pretended to be tea. Amanda was just grateful for something hot and sweet to cling to.

The boys filled in the details of what had happened as Amanda sat there sipping her tea.

"But who would do such a thing?"

"My dad has many enemies. The police spoke to us for hours, but they assure me they're investigating. At least they have the two attackers in custody."

Her drink finished, and the cup in the bin, the boys now sat either side of Amanda, taking a hand each.

She was resting her head on Mark's shoulder when a doctor came in.

"Michael is out of surgery. He's had a lucky escape so far. The bullet went through between his heart and lungs, missing them. There was of course internal damage, but we seem to have repaired the majority of it.

He's in intensive care, but his condition is stable. It's still serious though. Time will tell. We'll be monitoring him through the night."

Hugo translated for the others.

"Can we see him?" Amanda asked.

"He's still sedated at the moment. I suggest you go home for now, and we'll contact you if there's any change."

Amanda gasped as Hugo relayed this information. She had stood up as the doctor had entered, but she had to sit back down again now.

"Please. I have to see him," she begged.

The doctor consented to a very quick visit, with a warning that Michael was hooked up to machines.

She tried to brace herself, but as she got to the door she inhaled sharply. He was so lifeless. He was surrounded by all sorts of monitors, and tubes were sticking out of him.

She took a deep breath and went in on her own, the guys waiting at the door.

"Michael," she said softly. "I'm here, my darling."

She brushed his hand with hers.

"I know you're asleep, but I also know you can hear me. They won't let me see you long because you have to get your rest. But I couldn't not say hello to you. I'm going to a hotel with Hugo and Mark.

The doctors are going to let me know when you wake up, so I'll be right here, OK? Just wake up and I'll come running."

She delicately leaned over and kissed his forehead.

"I love you."

With a final squeeze of his hand she left him, she hoped not for the last time.

Mark caught her in his arms as she got to the door and fainted. He carried her out of the way and laid her down gently.

The doctor rushed through and took her pulse.

"*Is she pregnant?*"

"*No. I don't know. I don't think so,*" Hugo replied.

"*What's her name?*" Hugo told him.

"Amanda. Can you hear me?"

Her eyelids fluttered.

The doctor tried again, "Can you hear me, Amanda?"

"Yes," came the groggy response.

"Amanda. Are you pregnant?"

"I don't think so."

"When did you last eat?"

"Lunchtime, I think."

"OK. Take her to the restaurant, and make sure she eats and drinks before you go anywhere," he instructed Hugo.

"But bring her straight back if it happens again."

"Will do. Thanks."

He turned back to Amanda as the doctor departed.

"Food; doctor's orders. Do you think you can get up?"

She got up on shaky legs.

"Sorry," she apologised.

"No need to apologise. Right, I'm going to guess you don't want to eat here?" Mark questioned.

"Not if I can help it. Is there somewhere decent nearby?"

"Yeah. We'll find you something. What do you fancy?"

"Honestly? I'm not really hungry. I can't think about eating. But if I have to eat, I guess just a McDonalds will do."

"Your wish is my command, step this way."

And he helped steady her as they headed towards the exit. She stopped as they approached the door.

"Mark. How do we know it's safe?"

"Because you're with me."

"No offense, but…"

"OK. We're back on home turf. We're safe because I have some backup out there."

"Really? Or are you just saying that?"

"Are you kidding? After today, I called in extras, and ones we know and trust."

"OK then."

As they made their way outside Mark made a phone call.

"Dude, where's the car?"

He listened to the answer before thanking whoever it was, and headed them in the right direction.

The chauffeur was standing by the car, and doffed his hat at Mark. They were taken to a drive-thru, and ordered food, before being taken to their hotel nearby to eat their 'dinner'.

"I know it's not exactly the Ritz, but I'll sort something better tomorrow. It was the best I could do with short notice," Mark explained between mouthfuls of Big Mac.

"Mark?"

"Yeah?"

"Are we all sleeping in here?"

"Ummm…yeah. Sorry. I'm not separating us, and if anyone is still after Dimitri here they'll be casing the five stars."

"I get that, but there's only one bed."

"No, no. There's two. They're pushed close together, but there's two beds. I'll separate them more for you."

"So one of us has the floor?"

"That would be me. With the spare blanket and pillow. Yep."

"Mark."

"I've slept in worse places. It's fine. And I won't really be sleeping."

She went over and gave him a hug.

"Thanks."

"Least I can do."

When they'd finished their food Mark asked Amanda how she was feeling.

"I feel like shit. But if you mean am I going to faint again, then no, I think I'm OK."

"Well, thanks for the honesty," he smirked.

"Sorry. Bit blunt? I've just spent a week pining for my boyfriend, who is now lying in an ICU with tubes sticking out of him, having been shot today, and who may or may not survive the night. I haven't got an awful lot of energy for sugar coating pills."

"Hey. Come here," he said pulling her into a hug.

"Sorry, I'm not as good as Michael at this, huh?"

"I don't know. You're doing OK."

They finished their food, well, as much of it as they could manage. They'd all lost their appetite today. Mark got up and ran a bath for Amanda.

"Come on. This is for you," he commanded.

"No."

"No arguments."

She grabbed a change of clothes from her case and headed into the bathroom.

The water was perfectly hot, and actually quite welcome. She'd travelled a lot today, and felt dirty because of that, and the water revived her a little.

But visions came into her head as soon as she closed her eyes. Images of Michael lying helpless in that hospital bed haunted her.

She lathered the soap over her, pausing as she reached her breasts, recalling their booty call. 'Imagine I'm sucking them' she heard him say. She smiled as she thought about that moment, of all the moments he'd licked her there.

Would he ever do that again? She rinsed the soap off, and shampooed her hair. Memories of their shower together flooded her mind; of how she'd tugged him off, of him running his hands through her hair. She'd give anything to do that again.

She ducked her head under the water to rinse the shampoo out. She quickly got out of the bath, trying to run away from the memories she couldn't face right now.

Their former happiness was jaded by her current despair. She quickly towelled herself dry, and changed into her PJs.

She wandered back into the bedroom where the guys were sitting on the edge of the bed, staring into space. She'd rushed out of the bathroom craving their company, but looking at them, she wasn't sure they were in any better shape than she was.

"Some day, huh?" she commented, just to break the silence, as she sat down between them.

"I've had better," Mark confessed. "It's the day we all hope never happens. You know what my best day was?"

"Nooo."

"The day I met Michael."

"Huh. Mine too."

"I mean it. When I first met him I was on the verge of being evicted. I had no job, no money and no friends. I was drinking the last of my funds away in a bar. I was spoiling for a fight and I got one. Some big thug was beating ten kinds of crap out of me when Michael came by and pulled him off me.

You should have seen him. The guy was twice his size, but he picked him off like a piece of lint. The guy stalked off. And Michael just came up and reached out his hand. In that moment he saved me. He pulled me to my feet and asked if I was OK. I laughed at him through my swollen lips and made a smart Alec remark about did I look alright. He laughed back and took me back into the bar.

He grabbed some ice from the ice bucket, and led me through to the gents. He washed the blood of my face and held up a makeshift ice pack to my nose (which was bloody but somehow not broken).

He looked me up and down, and asked me for my story. He offered me training. He said he reckoned anyone spoiling for a fight with someone that size had the balls to work with him. So that was that. I trained hard, and got my life back on track. Been working with him ever since."

"You followed a strange bloke into a gents in a bar?" Amanda mocked.

"Hey. He'd just saved my arse, I kinda hoped he wasn't going to try to shag it. OK?"

"Ahh. Please," Hugo interjected. "I've seen the way you look at him. You wanted it."

"No. Fuck off you two."

But Mark was grinning.

"And what about you? Hugo. Dimitri. What's that all about?"

He looked at Mark.

"Dude. Her boyfriend just risked his life for you, and she's just flown all the way over here in a private jet she had no idea about. I think it's OK."

"OK." Hugo began. "Firstly, may I apologise?"

"Depends what you're apologising for," Amanda said slightly huffily.

"Hmmm. First, I apologise for where Michael is now. Second, I apologise for having lied to you and Claire. But we couldn't break protocol. If my name got out it may have been dangerous for us all. Too many people know it. My real name is Dimitri Krylov.

My father is a big shot energy baron. I'm ashamed to admit it. But there it is. He's rich, but I worry at what cost. It's certainly cost me my liberty. Years of shady deals has led to my current danger. When my father received death threats he employed Michael. Since then I've been known as Hugo outside my home. I even have a 'Hugo' passport and driver's license. So, it is sort of my name now. It didn't help today though, so again I apologise."

"Not your fault, man," Mark comforted.

"And it wasn't yours either," Amanda admonished.

They talked through the night, swapping 'Michael stories', recalling their happy times.

None of them could sleep; they didn't even bother trying. They just huddled together, offering comfort through their words, trying to 'hold it together'.

Mark held a strong arm around Amanda's shoulders for a lot of the time. She appreciated the strength. She knew there was absolutely nothing sexual in the contact.

They were just getting through the night in any way they could, dreading the phone ringing yet praying for it at the same time. They just wanted to hear he was alright.

Chapter 10

In the morning Hugo and Mark took it in turns to run themselves under the shower before they all headed out for the hospital.

Wary of another fainting episode, Mark got the driver to go via McDonalds again, so they could eat some sort of breakfast in the car on the way. They went to the ICU, where a man in a suit was standing.

"Hi Dean."

"Hi Mark. Long time no see."

The guys clasped hands.

"Yeah. Thanks for coming though."

"Anything for the Big Man."

"How's he doing?"

"Well, nobody has approached with a gun, so that's a good sign."

"Too soon."

"Sorry, you're right; not funny. Medically, I don't think there's any change particularly. The nurses have been doing their regular checks."

"Thanks."

They walked over to the nurse's station to ask for a progress report. The good news was he hadn't deteriorated. He was stable. The doctor was due soon to do his morning checks, so they went to the family room to wait.

It was only an hour, but it might as well have been all day to the trio in that room, but at last the doctor popped his head in.

"We've taken him off the ventilator, and removed his chest tube. He is breathing on his own. There is no sign of infection, but he's on antibiotics to make sure. He's looking a lot better than he did last night. He's healed incredibly well, actually. We'll be moving him to a ward today. We've stopped the sedation, so he'll be waking up soon."

Hugo again played interpreter. Amanda smiled, and let out a breath she hadn't realised she'd been holding.

"You can see him now," he told her.

She kissed his cheek and virtually ran through to Michael's bedside. The nurse was still there, clearing the equipment and monitoring him.

"He is just waking up. Give him time. He'll be sore and groggy despite the pain meds," she explained.

Amanda smiled her thanks, and held her boyfriend's hand. She stroked his matted hair. She felt a slight squeeze on her hand, and she almost jumped for joy.

"Morning, beautiful," she cooed.

He let out a stifled moan; a mixture of joy and pain.

"Shh…" she soothed.

"It's OK. No rush to speak. You just take your time. You're in hospital, but you're OK now."

"Hmmmm..?" came the questioning groan.

"It's OK. Wake up when you're ready."

His eyelids fluttered as he tried to open them; they just felt so heavy. But he was sure that was Amanda's voice. He wanted to see her.

He squeezed her hand again; that was easier. And he was reassured by the touch. She was actually here. Wherever the hell here was.

He'd got back to Moscow, right? So how was she here? He was so confused, and had so many questions, but he couldn't seem to move his mouth to formulate the words, no matter how hard he tried.

But what was that? Ahh, he felt Amanda's lips on his. That was nice. He moaned again, but this time more with pleasure.

"You like that?" Amanda's voice asked him.

"Mmmm…" he replied.

He felt her lips on his again. With a monumental effort he managed to open his eyes long enough to see hers glistening with tears and love. He had to close them again though. Damn it.

"It's OK. You'll wake up. Don't rush."

The nurse was smiling at the pair of them. She really liked a happy ending. She just hoped there wouldn't be any complications on his road to recovery. She pointed to a jug of water on the bedside table.

"He can have some of that. Just little sips though."

"OK thanks."

And the nurse wandered off on her rounds, satisfied that this patient was OK for now.

Michael wriggled his toes, which had just come back to life. Son-of-a-bitch! What the hell was on his chest? A cast iron safe? He winced as he tried to move.

"Uh ahh. Slowly. Gently. Naughty boy," Amanda told him.

"Amanda?"

There. He'd managed a word. And what a lovely word.

"Yes, it's me. Now, will you shut up and lie still?"

"Why?"

"Oh for chrissakes. Because you're in hospital. You got shot in the chest yesterday, and are just coming round after being sedated all night."

"Oh," he rasped.

It didn't take him too long to come round properly, but along with that came a whole wall of pain.

Amanda waved the nurse over, who administered more painkillers. Together, they shifted him up on the pillows enough so he could take a sip of water, with Amanda holding the glass for him.

"Better?" she asked.

"Mmm. Thanks."

"You'll be wheeled through to a ward soon apparently."

He looked around him.

"You're in ICU."

"That bad?"

"Yeah. Hugo was worried sick. He had me flown all the way over here. He thought you were dying."

"Ah."

"I'm very glad you're awake."

And she gave him another gentle peck on the lips before administering another sip of water. He went to take more, but she repeated the nurse's advice. He rolled his eyes. He really had to get a lot better very soon.

The porters came up to him, and shifted him onto a trolley as Amanda was shepherded back to the others.

Dean however, insisted on accompanying him. Michael looked up at him.

"Dean?" he asked doubting his senses.

"Yeah. It's me to the rescue."

"But?"

"But nothing. Mark lit the emergency flare last night and I was available to come play nursemaid. Nuff said."

"Thanks. Sorry."

"Shut up. You'll make me cry," he said sarcastically.

Michael could barely move. He just laid there as he was wheeled through the hospital, with his own personal guard. He was shifted into a bed, and was left with Dean.

"You know, they're not after me."

He was feeling a bit more up to conversation now.

"Yeah? 'I'm Spartacus'; ring any bells?"

"Oh."

"I'll take that as a yes. Bloody hero."

"Not."

"No. Idiot's more like it. What the fuck were you thinking?"

"That I might save my client?"

"Yeah, well I guess it worked."

"No offense, but where's Amanda?"

"What? You don't want to snog me?"

"Fuck off. Where is she?"

"She's on her way. Don't panic."

A few minutes later the lady in question walked up to him.

"Hello Superman."

"Don't. Please. Not you too."

"OK. But you'll get teased mercilessly once you're better. This is just a reprieve."

"Shut up and kiss me."

She bent in to obey, but he tried to grab her, which just sent pain ringing through his chest, making him yelp.

"Easy, Tiger. Bullet through the chest, remember?"

"Yeah. Not going to forget that in a hurry."

She bent in to kiss him, her hand on his arm to keep it lowered this time. As she stood upright two more faces surrounded her.

"Morning," Hugo and Mark chorused.

"No wisecracks?"

"Nah. Not yet. How you feeling?" Mark asked.

"Like I just got shot."

"Fair point."

"So, that was a close call?"

"Too close. Jesus, Michael. I thought you were fucking dying in front of me. There was blood everywhere."

"Sorry."

"Hell. I forgive you."

"So, someone like to update me how the love of my life is now in the danger zone?"

"The bad guys got arrested."

"Now, I know you're not *that* stupid."

"I called in the backup, and put her on the private jet. She's not left my sight, and won't."

"She smells of soap, she better have left your sight."

"Fuck off. You know what I mean. You ungrateful fucking…" as he ranted with many swear words Michael chuckled as much as he could before the pain cut him off.

"Cool it. I'm joking. I'm glad she's here. I know you won't let her come to any harm."

"You better believe it. We stayed in a hotel last night. Not quite sure about today yet."

"Have I taught you nothing?"

His anger was real now.

"I didn't have the keys to your bolt holes, genius. You moved them without telling me."

"Shit. OK."

He told Mark where to get the keys from. Just in time, as they got shooed out by the nurse soon after.

"I don't want to leave you," Amanda declared.

"I know. But you can't keep coming to see me here. It's too high a risk. Listen to me. Mark's taking you all to a safe place. At least until I can walk out of here. I have my guard, you stick with yours. Promise me."

"I promise," she agreed reluctantly.

"I just lost you twice in one week. I can't do it again."

"Which is why it has to be this way. I'll come get you just as soon as I can."

She kissed him again.

"Can I hug you without hurting you?"

"Probably not, but do it anyway."

She gave him the most delicate hug she could before kissing him once more before leaving with Mark and Hugo.

Dean sat down in the chair next to Michael's bed. The nurse glowered at him.

"I'm not a visitor," he declared, flashing his security ID at her.

"I wasn't aware he needed a security guard?" she said gruffly.

"Excuse me. I apologise for the oversight. I was on watch all night, I thought the ICU staff had told you."

"They didn't. Is he someone I should know?"

"No. Please do not concern yourself."

The nurse was now looking at two sets of enchanting blue eyes. The boys had joined forces in their innocent look.

"But he is very important. He was shot yesterday in a kidnap attempt."

"Oh. Is he OK here? Should he not be in a private room?"

The polite manners and endearing looks had softened her.

"Do you have a private room spare?" Dean's voice was sultry as he let his gaze lock onto hers.

"Yes if you help me move him there."

"That's very very kind of you."

The nurse blushed as they manoeuvred Michael into a secluded room. Once safely inside Dean reached for her hand and kissed it as he bowed.

"Thank you, Alyona."

She blushed more as he used her name as displayed on her name badge.

"Is there anything else I can get you?"

"No, not at the moment thank you, Alyona. There may be later though; may we call you if we do?"

"The patient buzzer is there," she said pointing. *"Press it and I'll come."*

"I like the idea of you coming as I press the right button. Thanks again."

The nurse flashed him a smile as she left them alone.

"I can't believe you just did that," Michael mused.

"What? Chicks dig me."

"Since when did your Russian improve so much anyway?"

"I've been out here a while now. It's been several years since we last worked together, you know."

"And you're sure you're not Soviet spy?" Michael said with that false accent and a wink.

"Man, I coulda killed you last night if I wanted."

Michael smiled, but the effort of talking had worn him out, and his lids grew heavy again.

"It's OK. Sleep if you want to. Do you want a bit more water first?"

"Would you mind? I feel a bit awkward asking you."

"Like you wouldn't do the same for me Big Guy?" Dean dismissed as he picked up a tumbler of water, putting a tissue under its lip as he lifted it to his friend's lips.

Michael took a couple of sips and laid his head back down. Dean lowered the back of the bed so Michael could get some sleep.

"Thanks," he muttered as he drifted off.

Dean allowed his mind to drift as he sat there, on guard. He thought of how this man, now lying invalid in a bed had given him his first assignment.

He'd previously been in the army, and was struggling on civvy street back in the UK. He'd managed eventually to get a job in a gym, which is where they'd met. Dean had spotted for Michael sometimes as he'd worked out.

They got to talking, and it had led to Michael offering him a job with him. He'd never looked back. He owed this guy a lot.

He was almost happy Mark had phoned him, he was now able to help him in return. He'd been on tenterhooks all night, as all he'd been able to do was watch on as the nurses did their checks. He'd been terrified he wasn't going to pull through.

The door opening had him pulling his head up with a jerk as he jumped to his feet in a defensive stance. Shit. Had he fallen asleep?

"Stand easy there," Alyona said softly. *"I'm just here to check his vitals, OK?"*

"Sorry, force of habit," Dean apologised as he sat back down, hitching up his trousers as he did so.

He watched in admiration as the nurse efficiently gave Michael the once over, and wrote some figures down on the chart on the end of the bed.

"Is he OK?" Dean asked tentatively.

"Yes. He's doing well. Some food will be here soon for him. Please make sure he eats it. I've ordered some for you too."

"Thanks. You didn't have to do that."

"Really? And how else are you going to eat?"

Dean looked almost bashful as he smiled at this lovely nurse.

"What time does your shift finish, Alyona?"

"Earlier than yours, I think."

But she smiled wryly as she once more left the room.

In the meantime, Amanda was pacing around the lounge of a two bedroom flat. The place wasn't great, but serviceable. And better than the hotel last night.

There were basic supplies in the cupboards, which they'd topped up with a whistle stop shop in a supermarket.

They were to be housebound for the rest of the week at least, so she was trying to make the most of it. But she was so worried about Michael. He'd looked so pale, and in so much pain. She just wanted to be by his side, helping him through this. But she was trapped here instead, not allowed to see him. She might as well be in her own sodding home.

Why the hell had she bothered coming all this way? But she knew the answer; she'd had to see him. To see with her own eyes that he was OK. And wild horses wouldn't have been able to keep her away.

Mark had switched the TV on, but it was all in Russian. She had no idea what was going on. Hugo was incredibly quiet.

"Amanda. Please will you just sit down, love?" Mark asked her sternly.

"You're wearing a hole in the carpet."

"I don't know what else to do."

She'd already phoned Claire, but her heart-to-heart hadn't really helped. Claire had said all the right things, but she just felt so restless and helpless all at once.

As she persisted in her pacing Mark stood up, and gripped her wrists in her hands, holding them low.

"He's OK. He's alive," he said as he looked at her directly in the eyes.

"I know. I know. I just want to see him, Mark."

"You can't. You heard what he said. Do you want to put him in danger? Let him get shot again?"

"No. Of course not."

"Then deal with it. You think I don't feel as defunct as you do? That I don't hate that it's Dean standing by him, not me? That I don't think my place is there? But pacing is not going to help."

"I'm sorry. But what *is* going to help?" she cried.

"I can't just sit here. But I'm not allowed out. I'm not allowed to be with Michael. I can't breathe."

She was crying bitterly now. Mark mellowed and pulled her into his arms.

"I'm sorry. I'm sorry. I didn't mean to snap at you. I'm just frustrated too."

He stepped back, and rubbed her upper arm soothingly. He walked into the kitchen and pulled out a bottle of vodka and three shot glasses, and offered them round.

"To Michael's health," he toasted, and they all downed their shots.

It was the only one Mark allowed himself, but it took the edge off his own jangling nerves.

"Well, when all else fails…" he suggested.

Amanda and Hugo slammed another shot. Mark grabbed the remote control and started channel hopping. He got to a movie channel.

"Die Hard baby!" he cheered, and flicked on the subtitles.

How did you spell 'yippee ki yay', he wondered? At least Amanda looked a bit better now. He really felt bad for her; she was in a strange country to her, where she didn't speak the language, away from her friends and family, not able to see her wounded boyfriend who was lying in a hospital bed, cooped up with him and a kidnapper's target. What a mess.

Michael was twitching in his sleep. Then he was yelling, almost screaming out. He yelled in pain as he tried to sit up from his nightmare. Dean was by his side.

"Hey there. It's OK. You're safe. You're safe."

Michael looked up from his sweat ridden face, his hair slicked down. He felt so stupid.

"Sorry."

"No. No apologies. Anyone would have nightmares after what happened to you. Here have some more water."

Dean lifted the tumbler up to Michael's trembling lips.

"You're getting too good at doing that," Michael commented.

"Don't get too used to it. You'll heal soon enough. You know you're one lucky bastard?"

"Yeah, feels that way," he sneered.

"That bullet fractured your ribs as it entered, but passed between your heart and lungs before coming out the other side. It could have been a hell of a lot worse."

"Yeah. That's what it feels like."

The door opened again and the food was brought in. The nurse walked up to the side of the bed.

"I'm not going to lie; this is going to feel very uncomfortable, but it's important you sit up. So, we're going to slowly bring your legs over the edge of the bed, and you're carefully going to stand up, and sit in that chair, OK?"

"Any more pain meds before I do?"

"Sure, here," Alyona said as she passed him some tablets.

She handed him the glass but made him drink for himself. It hurt like a bitch, but he managed.

"OK? Ready?"

"Uh huh."

It took ages, and a lot of wincing, but eventually Michael got himself into the chair. Alyona pushed the trolley over to him, so he could then eat. Dean had already tucked into his food as he watched Alyona help Michael into the chair. It really had looked painful.

"Just make sure you sit there this afternoon. I'll be back again later to check on you," she said kindly as she gave Michael his antibiotics to take when he'd finished eating.

"Are you warm enough?"

He nodded. She'd already put a blanket over him. He waited until Alyona had left before grumbling,

"I feel like an old man. Herded into a chair, wrapped up in a blanket, eating this muck."

"Stop whining, you're alive, aren't you?"

Michael agreed, and flicked the TV on.

"I'm not going to sleep whilst I'm sat here. Why don't you catch forty winks? You can even use my bed if you want?"

A grateful Dean accepted the offer. He got up on the bed, fully clothed and let himself fall asleep. He'd not slept since getting here, and he'd been up the entire day before too. Add to that the worry he'd been through last night; he was exhausted.

When the nurse came back a few hours later, Dean was still asleep on the bed. Michael held up a finger to his lips to warn her to be quiet.

"He's not supposed to be there," she whispered.

"I wasn't using it. Do you know the last time he slept?" he replied just as quietly.

Alyona took some blood and checked his responses.

"How are you feeling?"

"It still hurts a lot. And I'm really tired."

"OK. Let's get you back in that bed."

"Please. Not yet."

"You're the one who's been hurt. You need the sleep more than him."

"Fine."

He let the nurse wake Dean up.

"It's time for the patient to get back in there."

"You sure you wouldn't like to join me instead?" Dean said through bleary eyes.

She tapped him on the upper arm in mock astonishment.

"Come on. Up."

Dean obeyed, and helped Michael back into the bed.

"So, what time does your shift end?"

"Half an hour ago."

"But you're still here."

"Well noticed. You are observant. You must be very good at your job."

But she slipped a piece of paper with her phone number on into his pocket.

"For when you finish your shift."

The rest of the night passed in silence. Michael carried on sleeping, and a different nurse came and did her checks.

Dean tried watching TV; it was on, but he didn't pay much attention to it. He was lost in his own thoughts.

Amanda threw herself on the bed in 'her room' that night; exhausted with emotion, she finally managed to get some sleep. Mark had called the hospital and received updates on the patient.

The next morning Dean answered the mobile phone ringing on the bedside table.

"Hello?"

"Dean? It's Amanda. Is he awake?"

"Hello?" An excited Michael had managed to take the phone from Dean.

"Michael, you're there. You OK? How you feeling?"

"All the better for hearing you, Pretty One."

"I miss you."

"I miss you too."

"I don't know what do with myself. I think I'm driving Mark mad."

"I'm sure he's seen worse."

"Can I come to see you? I know you said no, but I can't bear this."

"It's too dangerous. I wouldn't be able to live with myself if I put you in danger."

"This is killing me."

"I know. I'm sorry. I'm trying to get better for you. The nurse made me sit in a chair yesterday."

"Ouch. Is she sadistic?"

"No. Apparently it's for my own good."

"Are you sitting up again now?"

"Yes."

"What are you wearing?"

"A hospital gown, naughty girl," he smirked.

"So, no underwear?"

"Stop it," he warned softly.

His cock was already poking its head up, eager for instruction and use.

"I'm sat on my bed."

"Amanda. Seriously. Dean's here."

"I'm sat here, naked. Just waiting for your return."

"Now you're just being cruel."

"Just giving you an incentive to get better and come get me."

"Amanda, you're there. That's all the incentive I need. Trust me."

"OK. I'll leave you in peace. But you be good, and do what the nurses tell you."

"Always. Love you."

"Love you too."

Amanda was smiling as she put the phone down. He sounded a lot more alert. This was good.

Dean was making kissy faces at Michael, "I love you smoochy coo."

"Fuck off."

"I want you. I need you."

"Fuck off."

"Come get me, lover boy."

Michael tried to rise to his feet but collapsed back down in pain.

"OK. Sorry. You OK there?"

"No. Fuck, that hurts," he growled in frustration.

"I need to get out of here."

"Not yet you don't."

"Aaargh, this is driving me crazy."

"Crazy's good."

Michael ate his lunch enthusiastically that day. He was famished. But the energy it gave him just made him feel like a caged tiger.

"Dean, to me," he commanded and was obeyed.

Michael leant on Dean's shoulder as he eased himself out of the chair.

"There," he said triumphantly as he stood up on his own.

He held his arms out as he took a very unsteady step forward with a wince.

He tried his other foot; that was easier; it was on his uninjured side. Hmph! Maybe should have started with that foot? He tried another step but plummeted into Dean's arms.

"Fuck," he shouted.

"Shh. It's OK. You were doing well. Come. Try again."

Dean said as he propped him back up. He held onto his arm this time, as Michael shuffled along.

He got to the bathroom, where he even managed to relieve his bladder on his own. He shuffled back out to an awaiting Dean.

"OK soldier. Let's not push this," he said as he led him back to the chair.

Michael sat down, exhausted. His frustration was written across his face.

"Do you know what you've just been through, arsehole? Do you have any idea how lucky you are to be walking at all? Don't you dare give me that look," Dean barked.

"Alright. Keep your hair on. You got issues you want to discuss?"

"Just be grateful, that's all."

"I am. Trust me, I really am. But I'm not going to sit here to be an easy target."

"And that's good. But celebrate your achievements. What you just did was amazing. You had a hole put through your chest, and your ribs were pretty hammered, and your leg got mashed as you hit concrete."

"OK. Fine. But I still want out."

"And you will. Patience, Michael."

Michael got himself back up on the bed, and slept that attempt off. This walking lark had suddenly got very tiring.

He kept trying all afternoon; walk, sleep, walk, sleep becoming his routine.

A nurse came to check on him as he was trying to walk again. Dean smiled as he realised it was Alyona back on duty.

"Well, someone's looking very determined," she commented.

"Determined is one word. Stubborn would be another. He's talking about getting out of here."

"Well, given he's doing so well, I'd say he could realistically achieve that in a few days."

"I'm right here," Michael interjected. "You can talk to me."

"Grumpy is also a good sign, I think," the nurse smiled at him.

"I wish all my patients impressed me this much. Just don't overdo it. Those wounds are still mending."

"Do you see me doing push-ups?"

"I'm sorry about him," Dean apologised.

"Don't be. I've heard a lot worse."

After doing her checks she left them alone again.

After dinner Michael picked up his phone.

"I'm not sure you should be using that in here," Dean warned.

"I'm not near equipment, its fine." Michael ignored him, and carried on dialling.

"That better be my boyfriend," Amanda answered.

"It is. Who else would it be?"

"Henchman Number Two."

"No. He's sat in the corner like a good dog."

Dean let out a mock bark at the comment. Amanda heard and laughed. It was so good to hear her laugh.

"I walked today," Michael informed her, sounding like a proud toddler.

"Well done. You're OK though? Did it hurt?"

"Lots. But it's worth it if it means I get to see you sooner."

"Just don't damage yourself."

"You sound like the nurse now."

"She must be a very wise woman."

"Not nearly as beautiful as you though."

"I wish you were here. I just want to hug you."

"I want to do more than that."

"Hmm…that may have to wait a bit longer, I fear."

"You kidding me?"

"We'll see. So, how long do you think it will be?"

"Nurse says a matter of days, but I'm working on it."

"Just don't rush. I don't need you dying of infection or anything."

"I'll be good."

They rang off after talking some nonsense. It was just so good to hear her voice.

He kept up his routine for the rest of the day, the phone call having spurred him on more. He slept really well that night though, having tired himself out.

Amanda, Hugo and Mark were still anxiously waiting in the flat. Everything they'd heard had been positive, but it was still a waiting game.

Mark was constantly on edge. He really wanted to get Hugo out of the country, but he daren't risk it yet. And he wasn't going whilst Michael was in hospital. He couldn't abandon him. He had barely slept; constantly vigilant for any slight sound that could be mistaken for an intruder.

Michael woke up screaming from his nightmare again that night. The gunshot was still ringing in his ears as he woke up. But Dean was on hand to calm him down again. The guy had been through a serious trauma; it was going to take time to get over it mentally as well as physically.

Things felt better in the light of the morning though. Michael managed to eat all his breakfast, and was soon pacing around his room.

By the time lunch came he was much steadier. He asked the nurse what his status was as she did his checks. She confirmed there was improvement. But when he asked to be discharged she told him she'd have to ask the doctor.

The doctor arrived an hour later, but told Michael that although he was improving, he should wait another two days before leaving.

"Fuck that," Michael stormed. *"Get me a wheelchair, and get me out of here now."*

"Be reasonable. If he says wait you wait," Dean tried to intervene.

"The hell I do. I'm healing. There's no infection. I'm walking."

"You're not walking, you're shuffling. You can barely go ten steps without rest. Michael, you've been through a lot. Don't do this."

"Your friend's right. You're still susceptible to infection. Your wounds are healing well, but they could still tear if you do too much; there could be internal bleeding."

"I have a job to finish."

"Work? You should not be working for another fortnight yet. You need to let yourself heal." The doctor advised.

"Mr Alkaev. You were shot just two days ago."

"I know. I was there," he was shouting now.

"Forgive me, my friend," Dean said as he hit him across the face.

"Fuck," Michael exclaimed as he tried to retaliate.

"Call security," the doctor called out to the nurse.

"We are security," Dean remarked.

Michael roared as pain ripped through him as he tried to swing a punch at Dean.

"Fuck. Shit, man. Fuck," Michael cried out.

"So, now will you listen? You CANNOT do your job like this, shithead!"

Michael stalked up to the wall, and with his good hand punched it.

"Hey! Hospital property, man. Not cool."

"Better that than your face."

"Granted, but will you calm down? You're upsetting your doctor."

Michael had the decency to look ashamed of himself, *"Sorry."*

"On the bed now," a rather agitated doctor ordered.

"You'll be lucky not to have ruptured something in that little macho display."

Michael was sweating and in immense pain as the doctor checked him over.

"I think you got away with it. But no more stunts like that. I don't think our walls could stand it."

"Is that a joke?"

"Yeah. I have a sense of humour, shoot me."

The doctor's face fell as he realised what he'd just said. The two boys just burst out laughing.

"Nice choice of words," Dean chuckled.

"Sorry. I didn't mean it like that," the doctor apologised whilst smiling too.

"Look. I'm really sorry about before. I just really have to get out of here." Michael said.

"I'm not your prison guard. I can't keep you here. But I can tell you you'd be crazy to go yet. I'll be back tomorrow though. Just keep taking your meds and get plenty of rest, and I'll review it then, OK?"

"Sure. Cool. Thanks."

"You fucking moron," Dean started as soon as the doctor had left.

"You want to delay your recovery? Just keep doing that."

"I said I'm sorry."

"You could have seriously hurt yourself."

"I know. I'm sorry, OK? I'm sorry."

"Talk about babysitting. Bloody tantrum throwing two year old."

"What do you want from me? I said sorry already. I got frustrated. I'm not used to being unable to do shit. And I've still got a high alert on my radar."

"I get it. Just cool it."

"I'm cool. I promise."

Michael slumped back on his bed and sulked. He flicked on the TV and zoned out for a while.

Dean dragged him to his feet later, and started him on his exercise regime again.

Things weren't much better at the flat. Mark was going stir crazy, Amanda was tearing her hair out, and Hugo was just sullen.

They were all anxious for Michael to recover quickly. But for now, all they could do was try their best to be patient.

"*OK,*" the doctor assented the next afternoon, having checked his latest tests and stats.

"*OK. You can go now. But no lifting anything. No physical exertion of any kind. Keep taking your meds, and promise me you'll rest.*"

"*Thanks. You sure it's OK?*"

"Anyone else, I'd say stay in longer. But you are physically fit, and you've been responding well to treatment. And I don't think you'd listen if I said otherwise anyway. Just take it easy."

"Got it. Thanks."

Chapter 11

Michael was making phone calls as he got wheeled to the front door.

Dean had had fresh clothes brought in, so at least he was dressed. One of their colleagues had driven his car up as close as he could. He hopped out and helped him get in the car, whilst Dean replaced him in the driver's seat.

"Thanks man," Dean said as he prepared to pull away.

The driver hopped into a car which had pulled up behind, which fell in behind as they drove out of the hospital. Another car joined in front of the procession.

They pulled up to the flat.

"Wait here," Dean commanded.

But Michael was in no condition to argue. He didn't want to walk anywhere right now, and besides, he was helping to keep a lookout down here whilst Dean brought the others downstairs.

Amanda lunged into the car, and wrapped her arms around Michael as carefully as she could.

"Michael, I'm so glad to see you," she said as she kissed him.

The others got in the car, and they zoomed off as quickly as they could.

Half an hour later they reached the airfield. They all piled out the car. Dean let Michael hang off his shoulder as they walked up to the plane, but he was going painfully slowly no matter how hard he tried to hurry.

"Mate. Sorry. This isn't going to be dignified," he said as he scooped him up in his arms and carried him the rest of the way, not putting him down until they were on board.

"Thanks Dean, for everything."

The two men locked arms as Dean left.

Mark shut the cabin door, and they were soon taxying up the runway. Hugo's dad's jet had been on standby for them. Michael looked pale as he chucked more pain killers down his throat as they took off.

"Are you sure you should be doing this?" Amanda asked in concern.

"I'm doing it," Michael's jaw was set in grim determination.

Shit. If this was him better, she was suddenly glad she hadn't been with him the last few days. She held his hand for the whole flight, but nobody said anything.

Amanda wasn't even sure where they were going. She was a little surprised when they touched down in the same airfield she'd left earlier that week.

A chauffeur was standing by a car at the entrance. Poor Michael. He limped his way over to it. Mark was sticking close to Hugo, so he couldn't help. And Amanda was carrying luggage. It was the pilot, Henry, who caught up to him and offered a supporting shoulder. Michael practically fell into the car.

"Amanda," he wheezed. "Tell the driver your address."

"What? I have a one bedroom flat. We won't all fit."

"Just do it, Pretty One," he said closing his eyes, leaning his head back on the headrest.

They headed off, but Amanda had to ask, "Are you sure we shouldn't be going via the hospital? You don't look right."

"No arguments. No detours."

Unable to argue, the car travelled on towards the flat.

"You'll be safe here. They don't know you, and they'll have no idea where Hugo's gone."

He let them get out the car, but didn't follow.

"I think I need the hospital, Jeeves," he said to the chauffeur (whose name was actually Paul).

He raced through the traffic, really not liking the look of his passenger's colour.

He pulled up to A&E and flagged down an orderly, who whizzed a wheelchair round. Paul filled him in on as many details as he'd been told about his passenger before leaving him there (at Michael's request).

Michael got wheeled straight in to an exam room. A doctor checked him over.

"Does it hurt here?" she checked.

"Yeah."

"Here?"

"Aaargh!"

"OK."

She started barking orders at the nurse.

"I'm getting you to X-Ray now. I just want to be sure there's no internal haemorrhaging."

Michael found himself on yet another hospital trolley, but he was just grateful for the help. He was suffering immense pain, and was sweating profusely. A doctor looked at his scans.

"Well, you look clear."

"That's good, right?"

"You'd think so, wouldn't you?"

"So, what's the trouble?"

"Possible secondary infection. What meds were you given?"

Michael pulled out the bottles of tablets from his jacket and handed them over.

"OK. We'll increase your dose of this one, but these you can have back," the doctor said, passing back the painkillers.

"When was the last time you took some of these?"

"About four hours ago?"

"Good. Take a couple more now," the doctor ordered, handing him a glass of water.

"I'm going to admit you overnight, more for observation than anything. I want to make sure that fever of yours comes back down. Presuming it responds to your improved antibiotics you'll be good to go in the morning."

"Thanks doc."

Michael let his head collapse on the trolley he was now on.

"Can I make a phone call?"

"Not in here. But once you're on the ward and wait until nobody's looking I'm sure a quick one won't hurt," the doctor winked.

"Do you think you can stand for me?"

Michael obeyed, very slowly.

"Well done. Plonk yourself in here," the doctor patted the seat of a wheelchair.

"You'll be fine. You're in good hands."

And with that an orderly wheeled him through to a ward. With a little help, he managed to get up on the bed.

He quickly fired off a text to Amanda, letting her know which ward he was on, and confirming he should see her in the morning.

She was frantic. Ever since he'd been driven off without a word she had visions of him not surviving. He'd looked so ill. Why had he come out of hospital so soon?

Michael swallowed his new antibiotics having managed to eat a few mouthfuls of dinner, and laid back down. The room felt like it was spinning, but he soon fell into a fevered sleep.

He didn't wake up until the next morning, with someone nudging him awake, alerting him breakfast was being served. He ate his porridge like a good little Goldilocks, and took more antibiotics and painkillers.

He felt dreadful, like he'd been on an all-week bender. A nurse came and checked his pulse and temperature.

"How are you feeling?" she asked.

He replied in the negative.

"OK. Rest here and I'll ask a doctor to stop by in a bit."

He let his head fall back down. The next thing he knew a doctor was waking him up.

"What?" he asked drowsily.

"Ah. You're feeling that good, are you? Mind if I just check you over?"

"Go ahead."

"Can you sit up for me?"

Michael winced at the effort, but managed. The doctor shone a light in his eyes, making him shy away.

"Hmmm…follow this pen with your eyes for me."

Michael obeyed, but it made his head swim a bit. The doctor looked at his notes.

"OK. I'll stop by again after lunch."

"Sure. Thanks."

He wasn't fighting this time. He was going to follow advice. Hugo and his Amanda were safe now. That's all that mattered.

He sent off a text update and fell back asleep.

He was woken up by the food trolley; his prompt for more meds. At least he could feel the painkillers kicking in. And he felt less hot now. He managed half of his lunch, but drank lots of water.

He dozed until the doctor came round, as promised. He was assessed.

"Your temperature's coming back down, and you're looking a lot better. But I'd rather keep you in overnight. The nurse tells me you've been asleep all day. That's good, you need rest. But can you try sitting up in this chair for me?"

As Michael shifted his weight the room started spinning again.

"It's OK. Take it slowly," the doctor told him.

Michael managed to get in the chair.

"What? No TV?"

"Only if you want to pay for it."

"I'll pass thanks."

As he was left on his own, staring at the blank wall opposite, Michael wished Dean was still guarding him. Anything for a bit of distraction. His head was thumping, and (not that he'd admit it to anyone else) he was a little scared.

A big bunch of flowers and a bunch of balloons came walking through the ward. Michael peered through his foggy haze.

"Hello hero," Amanda cheered.

She set the flowers on the side and settled the helium balloon's weight on the floor next to him. She sat down sideways on his lap.

"Is this OK?" she checked, not wanting to hurt him.

"Yeah."

He wrapped a heavy arm around her waist, and leaned his head on her breasts.

"Poor baby," she soothed, as she stroked his hair.

He still looked a bit pale, but not as awful as the last time she'd seen him.

"How you feeling?"

"I've been better. Glad you're here though. Do you know they charge for TV in these places? I've been told to sit in this chair, with only a blank wall to stare at."

"Are you able to sit on the edge of the bed for a sec?"

"I think I can manage that."

Amanda moved his chair over to the window and went to fetch him. "Can you make the walk all the way over there?"

"Hmmm…are you going to help me?"

"If you wish."

She offered him her arm.

"Slowly slowly catchy monkey."

Michael laughed at her.

"What? You never heard that?"

"Errr…no."

"Well, just take things slowly."

Oh, how he'd missed that smile. He got to his feet, slowly as instructed, and shuffled towards the chair, leaning on her arm.

Amanda fetched another chair and put it beside his. She also brought over a glass of water for him.

"Can you drink on your own like a big boy?" she teased.

"Yes thank you," he replied, taking a sip, just to prove he could.

"It's OK. You're still beautiful, even when you're sick," Amanda chided.

"Thanks. Good to know," he half smiled.

It was nice to have a view out the window, but the view to his side was far far better.

"I missed you," he admitted.

"I missed you too."

She gave him a peck on the lips. They sat there quietly, just enjoying being near each other.

"Ummm…Amanda?"

"Yes?"

"I have a problem."

"What?"

"I need to go to the toilet," he said shyly.

"We talking bottle or a long walk?"

"Errr…you OK to help me go the distance?"

"You may need more specialist help for that."

She went and asked a nurse. He was escorted to the loos.

He came shuffling back soon, where Amanda was still looking out the window.

"Sorry about that."

"Not a problem."

"You look like you're ready for a lie down again now though."

"Yeah."

She helped him to the bed. She moved one of the chairs back, but left one by the window, in case he wanted to return to it later.

"Lie down next to me."

"The nurse will throw a wobbly."

"Please."

How could she deny him? She snuggled up to his side, and laid a hand across his waist, staying clear of his bandaged chest. She felt good there.

A nurse came to announce visiting hours were over.

"Please. Please let her stay until I'm asleep. It won't take long."

The nurse narrowed her eyes, but she allowed his request.

And he was right, a few minutes later his steady breathing indicated his sleep. Amanda crept away, thanking the nurse on the way out.

"How is he?" she asked the professional.

"He's getting there. His signs are good. Hopefully you'll have him back tomorrow."

"Thanks."

Amanda drove home, and gave a full report. That night the trio all actually slept properly for the first time since the shooting.

Amanda was back at the hospital as soon as she could the next day. She was carrying a McDonald's bag.

"Thought you might prefer this?"

She offered her boyfriend the fast food. He was sat up in the chair by the window, where she'd left it. He was also wearing the pyjamas she'd bought him the day before. She'd had to stop off at the shops on her way to him, and had to guess his size.

"Thanks."

He ate the burger enthusiastically.

"Carefully. Don't give yourself indigestion."

"Amanda. Can you do me a favour, please?"

"Name it."

"My meds are on the table by my bed. Would you mind getting them for me, please?"

She dutifully brought them over, and he chased them down with his Coke.

"Thanks. It just seemed a bit far away."

"And how's our patient today?" the doctor called out as he walked up to Michael.

"Ahh. Up to visitors and junk food I see?"

"Ahem. Yeah."

"Well, you look a lot better. Let's see," he muttered as he read the nurse's notes.

He took Michael's temperature himself.

"OK. How do you feel about vacating that bed for someone who's really sick?"

"Do you mean it? I can go home?"

"No reason to keep you in. Keep taking this course of antibiotics until the end though. And come back in if you start feeling unwell again."

"Thanks."

Michael's face had lit up. He walked slowly back to the bed and Amanda drew the curtain round, so he could change into the jeans and T-Shirt she'd bought him. The T-Shirt fit alright, but the jeans were a little short.

"Sorry. I guessed a little wrong with those."

He reached out and hugged her.

"They're close enough. Thank you. Now let's get out of here. I am really bored of hospitals."

He signed the discharge paperwork on their way out. Amanda brought her car round for him, and they drove back to her flat.

A small cheer went up as they walked into Amanda's home. Hugo and Mark had put up a couple of banners and a few balloons.

"Welcome home, mate."

Mark grabbed Michael's hand. Hugo came up next, and patted him on the shoulder.

"Glad you're back with us."

"I'm glad to be back. But can I just head for that couch, please?"

The guys stood aside, and let him take a seat.

"So, what do you want to eat?" Mark asked.

"Have you got beans on toast in there?" he asked.

"Baked beans on toast coming up, sir." Michael pulled out his bottles of tablets and took them when he'd scoffed the comfort food down.

Mark had also made him a cup of tea, which Michael also drank.

"Ahh, now that's more like it," he sighed, as he put his feet up on the coffee table.

Amanda smiled as she cuddled up to him. He looked right at home, here in her lounge.

Amanda got up to answer the intercom.

"Hi, come on up."

She opened the door and let Claire in. Hugo rushed past and gathered her up in his arms.

"Claire. I've missed you."

She kissed him.

"I missed you too."

She hadn't appreciated just how much she'd missed him until this moment. She held him close before walking through to the gathering.

"How's the patient?"

"Much better thanks," the patient replied.

"Good. Then I can do this."

She whacked him on his good arm.

"What was that for?"

"For letting my friend break her heart over you. And that," (another whack) "is for getting yourself shot, making her heart break even more."

"Gee. Sorry."

"You're forgiven," she smiled as she kissed him on the cheek.

"Glad you're OK, idiot."

She then held Amanda in a cuddle.

"You've been through too much this week. You OK?"

"Yeah. I am now," Amanda replied, with a grateful sigh.

"So, what's the master genius plan then, Michael?" Claire asked.

"Right now, I plan on recovering."

"Here?"

"If I can, yes."

"And the two stooges over there will be staying with you?"

"That was the idea."

"In a one bedroom flat?"

"They're sharing the sofa bed."

"How cosy for them."

She dashed back to the hall, and came back dragging an inflatable mattress.

"This might be useful then?"

"Thanks Claire," a very grateful Mark piped up.

"It was a bit cosy for two on the sofa bed. There's close personal protection, and there's just too close."

"I have a sleeping bag too, but it's in the car downstairs."

Mark went and gave her a hand. She also had a few platters of party food for the little home coming.

"You're a very good friend to have, Claire." Mark couldn't help observing.

"Thanks. You're quite handy to have around too," she smiled at him.

"So, what are the future plans?"

"Honestly? I still don't know. Michael just got out of hospital take two. He needs to get a lot better before we can even start thinking of what next. I'm not risking him getting ill; I don't think my nerves can stand it. Unfortunately, Hugo is still under our remit, so I'm not going to break up our happy little family, so we're just making do with here for now. It's like I'm guarding him and Michael really."

"Sounds like you have your hands full."

"Yeah. But Amanda's here."

"Amanda has a day job."

"Yeah, I guess she ought to start doing that again, eh?"

"Unless she wants to find herself sacked it's probably a good idea. Our boss has been patient but that won't last forever. Her cover story was her uncle was in a car accident, by the way, in case anyone phones here.

The five of them were quite a merry party. Michael was happy just to be out of hospital, Amanda was ecstatic he was alive and by her side, Mark likewise was relieved, and Hugo had perked up all of a sudden.

They tucked into sausage rolls, sandwiches, cocktail sausages, cheese and pineapple, and all things classic party food.

When Michael looked like he was flagging Amanda took him into the bathroom. She stood close, supporting him as he had a shower. She washed his hair for him, and made sure he was clean all over. His grin became mischievous, but she curtailed that. This was strictly hygiene. But she was happy to have her hands running up and down him nonetheless.

She made sure he was carefully patted dry, and replaced his dressings. He was enfolded in a new towelling robe and led to the bedroom so she could dry his hair properly. Then, and only then, did she let him lie down for a well-earned rest.

"Don't leave me," he pleaded as she got up to go.

So she laid down on the bed next to him, stroking his refreshed hair and gently snuggled under his good arm.

"It feels so much better when you're there," he breathed.

"Yeah."

"I thought I was never going to see you again."

"Shhh…you're here now. That's all that matters," she soothed.

"I love you," he said softly, his eyes closing.

"I love you too."

A few minutes later his breathing had slowed, and Amanda crept quietly out of the room to re-join the others.

"How is he?" Mark inquired.

"Sleeping."

"It's OK, you know. He's still healing. He'll be sleeping a lot still."

"I know. I think it's all just sinking in now I've stopped."

Amanda felt Claire's arms around her as she lowered herself onto the sofa.

Claire disappeared into the kitchen, but came out a few minutes later carrying a tray of mugs of tea. She handed one to Amanda, who smiled.

"Always good in a crisis?" she quipped, raising her mug in the air a little.

The four of them talked quietly among themselves until a yell had Amanda and Mark running to the bedroom. Michael was sat up in bed, covered in sweat, a look of terror on his face. Amanda was by him in a second.

"Shh...it's OK," she said quietly, gripping his hand.

"You're safe."

He'd had the nightmare again, reliving that near fatal moment the gun went off. She went and got a damp flannel and wiped his face gently.

Mark had disappeared back into the lounge. Claire looked aghast, but he explained what had happened.

"Shit. Poor guy," was her only comment.

"Yeah. I've never seen him like this, but then I'd never seen him shot before either. Guess that would shit anyone up."

Amanda didn't leave Michael's side again until the morning.

"Time for me to go to work, baby," she said softly.

He groaned and tried to roll over to hold her there, but was forced to halt his progress as pain shot through him. He lied on his back with a grunt. Amanda's mouth was on his, consoling him.

"Don't go."

"I have to, unless you want to live out on the street."

And with a quick brush of his cheek, she went into the bathroom. She went back into the bedroom to get changed, where Michael had managed to sit up in bed.

"Come here first, Pretty One," he commanded as she was about to put on some underwear.

"I want to feel you first."

She sat on the edge of the bed, where he could put an arm around her and he nuzzled her.

"OK. You're real. You may abandon me now."

She took him a lap tray with tea, orange juice and toast before she left.

At work, Amanda went and reported in to her boss. She padded out the white lie Claire had started. What? She couldn't say, 'sorry, my boyfriend who I only just met on holiday was shot in the line of duty, and I had to fly to Russia as he could have died. Oh and went into hiding for fear of kidnappers'.

She did feel a tad guilty when some of her colleagues came up to her that morning and offered their get well wishes for 'her uncle' though.

The boys were still house-bound, thanks to Michael's injury, so Amanda and Claire went shopping on their way home. They bought a few changes of clothes (with amended sizes for Michael), and picked up some more food too (hitting Amanda's credit card hard, but the boys had promised a reimbursement). When they returned to the flat Michael was sitting on the sofa with the other two boys, watching DVDs.

"Productive day then?" she asked in mock irritation.

"Yes thank you," Michael said, his smile reaching his eyes again.

He was so much happier here, and the painkillers were helping, and the antibiotics seemed to be kicking in properly. He even managed to get up, wander over and kiss her.

"Have you been cooped up in here all day?" she asked.

He nodded at her.

"Here, try these on," she said, passing him a bag of clothes.

"Then we're going outside."

It was pleasantly warm outside; an almost perfect summer evening. The girls chucked the leftover party food in a cool bag with some fresh supplies they'd just bought.

They all headed out to the lush green park down the road. Amanda laid out a blanket and laid out their picnic dinner.

She held onto Michael's hands as he lowered himself down onto a rug. It felt really good to have the sun on his face, and the breeze waft through his hair. He could hear birds singing in the trees.

"I've not done this for years," he marvelled, his smile broad and beautiful.

The fresh air seemed to do them all some good. Mark and Hugo had a kick about with the ball the girls had also bought.

They'd been like battery hens this last week, so it was pure bliss to get out and get some exercise. Michael looked on, slightly enviously, but Amanda's lips soon made him realise he had the better end of the deal.

Michael went to bed when they got back to the flat, and Amanda followed. He reached up gingerly to bring her face to his. He kissed her, and his erection was immediate.

"Someone's feeling better," she smirked.

"You could make me feel a whole lot better," he leered as he tugged her onto the bed.

"OK. But we're going to take this slowly. If it hurts we're going to stop. Promise?"

"Promise."

So she helped him off with his clothes before disrobing herself. She straddled his hips as he lay there on his back.

"No sitting up," she warned him.

"You're just going to lie right there and let me do the hard work."

And she slid him into her, giving her hips a little wriggle in satisfaction. She'd missed this. Michael moaned in pleasure but didn't move. She tentatively started her up and down motion.

He felt her slickly massaging his cock, making him groan even more, but he kept still.

She planted her hands on either side of his head and bent down to give him a deep, passionate kiss, their tongues interlocking. She carried on, checking for signs of pain as she did. She only saw pleasure, so increased her speed. He felt so good.

Her need increased, and Michael was finding it nigh impossible not to move his hips, but she didn't notice. She was getting swept away as the first wave of her orgasm came crashing over her.

"I missed you," she panted.

His eyes were shimmering; that naughty, playful light finally back where it belonged. It spurred her on, and she carried on her ride.

She tried to steady herself, but had to give up, and let herself fall onto her arms by his head. Her hips were still pumping hard as she leaned in and sucked hard on his neck, making him groan loudly.

He couldn't resist any longer, and his hips jerked to meet hers. They rocked together, their climax just within reach. Onwards they pushed; it was closer now. She sucked again, and they came together. Michael groaning half in pleasure half in pain. But the pain just threw him further over the edge, coming out in an, "Argh…aaaarrrrgh!"

She brought her head up to his so she could kiss him more, before carefully climbing off, worried she may have hurt him. But he was OK. He was more than OK. He was where he belonged. He was happy.

Amanda wandered through the lounge in her bathrobe, and was received with cheers. She blushed wildly.

"Was it that loud?" she asked bashfully.

"No. I think some people in the next block may not have heard," Mark teased.

She scurried through into the kitchen to get the drinks she'd intended to get. She bit her lip and kept her head lowered as she walked back through, glasses in hand.

She got back to Michael who was grinning.

"Oops. Thin walls," he beamed.

He wasn't embarrassed. He'd let the whole world know how much he loved this woman if he could. This brave, strong, clever, beautiful creature.

That Sunday Amanda went to her weekly roast meal with her parents. It was the first time she'd made it there for a few weeks, given the holiday and the drama.

She had told her mum to expect guests, including a boyfriend. Her mum was delighted; finally, a boyfriend for her precious girl. And guests to fuss over. She got her husband to pull out the extension for the dining table, and the house was full of flowers fresh from their garden. The 'best' crockery and glasses adorned the table.

Amanda rang the doorbell, and held onto Michael's hand; it was hard to tell which of them was the most nervous.

"Amanda darling," her mum screeched as she threw her arms around her.

"I've not seen you for so long. Oooh, caught the sun, I see," she said, admiring her tan.

"And this must be your young man?"

"Mum, this is Michael. Michael, this is my mum."

"Audrey, please," she cooed as she hugged him, making him inhale sharply in pain.

"Oooh. Sorry. Are you OK?"

"Sorry. Yes. Just bruised ribs; holiday accident," he supplied the agreed line.

"Oooh, you didn't go on one of those dreadful banana boats did you? They're death traps."

"Something like that."

"Come in, come in. Here's me keeping you standing on the doorstep."

She led the way through to the sitting room. Amanda finished off the introductions to the other three, who were all hugged by her mother and had their hands shaken by her father.

"I didn't know what you all liked to drink, but I hope Sherry's OK," she said passing the aperitifs round the group.

"It's so lovely to have a full house. Please make yourselves at home," Audrey said excitedly as she whisked into the kitchen to dish up.

She soon announced dinner, and they were all herded into the dining room. Her father was at the head of the table on carving duty.

The plates of roast beef were handed round to all, who were then free to help themselves to the accompaniments laid out in their serving dishes. Amanda put the vegetables and gravy on Michael's plate for him.

"Oh, you poor dear," Audrey sympathised, noticing her daughter's assistance.

"I'm OK. Just a bit stiff and sore still," Michael tried to dismiss her concern.

"So, you all met on holiday?" Audrey started, as they all tucked into the feast.

Although details were kept to a minimum, Amanda's mother was captivated. Michael had such a lovely accent, and such polite manners; yes, her daughter could be very happy with that nice young man (providing he stopped his antics on banana boats).

They were fit to bursting after dinner. Mark and Hugo had managed the offered 'seconds', but were now sitting back in their chairs, feeling like they were about to pop the buttons off their shirts.

"That was delicious. Thank you Audrey," Michael said sincerely.

It made Amanda's mum blush slightly.

"You're welcome," she beamed.

"Why don't you all go out into the garden, and I'll bring some coffees out?"

Michael sat down in a wooden chair next to Amanda's father.

Amanda was shocked to hear her father say in a hushed tone to Michael, "Banana boat, my arse."

Michael looked slightly abashed.

"Sorry sir. Amanda thought it best not to tell her mother the whole story."

"Quite right. Quite right. No use upsetting the apple cart. Mind my asking though? What was really the mishap?"

"Something that's not ever going to happen again."

"Very good. Glad to hear it."

And he left it at that, content that his daughter was acceptably safe.

Audrey came out with a few large cafetieres, and handed round some coffee cups. It was rather lovely, sitting in the sunshine in that garden, and they chatted the afternoon away.

But it was soon time to go. Michael thanked her mother for her wonderful hospitality and she glowed with pride.

"Your parents seem really nice," Michael commented once they were safely on their way home.

"Yeah, they're OK. A bit full on though, sorry."

"It was very nice to have English hospitality," Hugo added appreciatively.

They had been so warm and friendly to them all. Even Mark agreed it was nice to be made so welcome, and confessed it had been many years since he'd had such a gorgeous, home cooked meal.

A few weeks later and you would hardly know anything had ever happened. Michael's wounds were now just scars, which in time would fade.

Michael had spoken with Hugo's father who agreed the safest place for his son was the UK for the foreseeable future, and gave him a monthly allowance and a large sum to get him a place to live.

He'd also given Michael a very generous reward as compensation for him taking a bullet to protect his son's life. It was more than enough to set him up for life, but he wasn't ready to be idle.

Once they were sure the coast was clear, and the threat of danger was minimal it was time to think of the future.

Hugo moved into a sumptuous penthouse apartment near the water. Mark had his own room there, as he was now the live-in guard, but they were more like flatmates.

Security was much more relaxed, and Hugo had now changed his name again, so really I should have said Joseph moved into a penthouse. His relationship with Claire seemed to be blossoming, and she was a regular visitor.

Amanda was nearing the end of her month's notice at work. Michael had more than enough money to support them anyway, and they were taking a well-earned rest whilst the centre he'd bought was being renovated.

They were both getting their qualifications to teach dance. Michael already had a qualification to teach self-defence so he was going to start teaching that first, and Mark was going to assist him. But it wouldn't be too long before they could start admitting girls in their pink tutus and boys in their leotards, eager to learn ballet.

They were just moving into their new house, not too far away from Joseph formerly known as Hugo. Life was good.

What? You want to know if there were wedding bells in the air? Of course there were.

As soon as he was properly mobile, Michael took Amanda out for a romantic meal. The daft fool made a very exaggerated show of getting down onto one knee (imagine a ballet dancer stretching out an arm, and taking a step forward with pointed toes as he folds down onto the floor; yeah that was it). Of course, it caught the attention of all the other diners, making Amanda laugh.

"Amanda," he declared.

"If I continued travelling the globe for the rest of my days I could not find another woman as wonderful as you. You are as beautiful as you are intelligent. You are so courageous, and have stood by me in my darkest hour, shining your light steadfastly. Amazing Amanda, please, would you make me the happiest man alive? Please, would you be my wife?"

The ring he held out had an emerald centre, hugged by a diamond on either side on a platinum band. It reminded him of that night in Ibiza, after they'd been out on the boat, and gone out to dinner. The night she'd dazzled him as if she was a star.

"Yes," she laughed.

"A million times yes. You are my true love, and I want my happily ever after."

No, Amanda Trueman didn't do dates. But she could do marriage.

Thank you for reading True's Love.

Please don't forget to rate it.

As an indie author I truly appreciate each and every review.

About the Author

Just in case you want to know about me, I (like some of my characters) have an office job to pay my bills. I have to squeeze my writing into the precious little free time I have.

I was born, raised and still live on the south coast of England.

I'm also an Equine Reiki Master (as well as being trained in other holistic therapies).

My dearest wish is to buy a farmhouse, so my husband and I (along with our spoiled cat) can run a retreat for those who are feeling frazzled by the stresses of the modern world.

So, that's me in a nutshell.

In love and light,

TL Clark

You can catch up with me on Twitter:

TLClarkAuthor

I'm also on Facebook, Goodreads or Instagram.

Other books by TL Clark:

<u>Young's Love</u>

Samantha's journey from doormat to independent woman, with a trip to Tuscany along the way. Will she find true love or just a love of gelato? Join her on her quest and find out.